MW00655832

The Vanishing

Book 1 of the Gamekeeper Saga

B.A. ACTON

Cover art by Dragan Paunovic

ISBN:
ISBN-13:

DEDICATIONS

Ann's Dedication: For Bret, Brittany, Brianna, Bethany, and Brenick.You will always be my greatest adventure.

Brenick's Dedication: For Chuck Norris. If he were in a Battle Book, the monsters would roll to defeat themselves

THE

VANISHING

BOOK 1 OF THE GAMEKEEPER SAGA

ACKNOWLEDGMENTS

First off, I'd like to thank my family. They put up with a lot of sacrifices to make this crazy dream of mine a reality. I'm sure more than once they've thought, "*Why can't she just take up knitting like a normal person.*"

Next, I need to thank the tireless efforts of my fantastic critique group. Terry Deighton, Stacey Nash, Michelle Wilson, Liz Adair, Christine Thackary, Tanya Mills, and Bonnie Harris. Your support and critiques have changed a lump of letters into something worth reading. Thank you for all your help and encouragement.

I'd also like to thank all the "advisory team" or family that I conned into helping A LOT. Savannah Acton, Gillian Gonzalez, Lisa Acton, Laurie, Robert, Ronin and Roberto Gonzalez, Scot Acton, Brianna Cruz, Bret and Chelsie Acton, Bethany Acton, Tom and Bobbie Muir, and Vickie and Bill LeMmon.

Last but not least, Brenick and I would like to thank all of the people who preordered the book. Especially those who pledged the Early Bird pledge in the Kickstarter campaign. Melissa McDonald-Rocco, The Dilley Family, Terese Becker Bartlett, Guest 1851711767, Tara, Joshua C. Hatfield, Barnett Children, New Path 57, Sarah, Josh, and Victoria Arquitt, Lisa Acton, Guest 1816208990, Joey, Mascio, Guest 671872508, Christine Critchley, V. Yeates Family, Nicole King, Guest 847087816, Sharon Storrs, Guest 674690144, Kammie Lintvedt, Unisus, Guest 87872274,Tary Taylor, Bonnie Harris, Candace Torgerson, Bonnie Smith, Jenny Gunn, and Lara Yates Niedermeyer.

Thanks to everyone who contributed. You may not be mentioned by name, but we hope you understand how much we appreciate you.

Warning:

This book is not like any other story you've read. Here, you are the main character. Your actions will determine how far you get. Only those with the skills to survive will make it to the end. Battle are determined by rolling a die at each battle page. With the right roll, you can also gain items that will help you in later battles. You will begin with 50 points, but in each fight, you could sustain damage that will deduct points. If your points reach zero, your story will end. Fight hard and good luck—you'll need it!

***

CHAPTER 1

Torture—that's what this is. Torture. You look back at your little sister trailing slowly along the path behind you. A large, beach towel drapes across her neck and tangles around her legs.

"Why are you so slow? Mom and Dad were probably like, 'Should we throw him into a pit of poisonous snakes? No, too humane. Let's make him walk somewhere with Ashley.' You're killing me."

"I'm walking as fast as I can," she says. "I'm only five."

You stop to let her catch up. "No, you were five when we started walking. Now we both need false teeth and a cane."

She finally catches up, and you walk side by side, but before long, she falls behind again.

Grabbing her by the arm, you drag her forward. "I swear, I'm going to leave you. Zack is already waiting."

"I'll tell Mom," Ashley says.

"Oh, like I've never heard that one before. You

can't tell her anything if I leave you here in the woods to rot." You start walking faster, pulling her along. She only drags her pink sneakers along the road even slower.

"I'm tired," she whines. "Can you at least carry my towel?"

"You're the one who wanted to come, Ashley. You begged Mom and Dad to let you go swimming with Zack and me. So, suck it up and get moving."

She looks up at you with her puppy dog eyes. Like always, you cave.

You take her towel and throw it over your backpack full of lunch stuff and extra clothes. She starts to walk faster. Soon, you see Zack waiting where the road splits into two paths.

"What's with the midget?" Zack says.

"Mom and Dad decided to let her come swimming with us. Something about family unity and a bunch of other gooey, feel-good stuff I tried to tune out."

You all turn down the fork of the road that leads toward the lake.

Zack laughs and takes a drink from a canteen

around his neck. "No big deal. Ashley's not so bad.

Ashley beams up at Zack.

"Oh brother, have you got a lot to learn about sisters," you say. "They're whiney and sneaky and—"

"I'm gonna tell Mom." Ashley whines and sticks out her lip.

"Oh, yeah, and then there's that. They always tell. *Always*!"

Zack adjusts his glasses. "You should try being an only child. Your parents only have one chance. If you turn out to be an axe murderer, they can't point to your sibling and say, 'I don't know what happened. Our other kid's perfectly normal.' It puts a lot of pressure on them to get it right. And, if you break something, forget about it. They know you did it. I finally had to talk them into getting me a dog, just so I could catch a break once in a while."

Now it's your turn to grin. "I never thought about that before."

The road parallels a piece of property that everyone in town knows is owned by Mr. Larsen, a grumpy old man with a bad leg. A huge chain link fence, dotted with private property signs and topped with razor wire, surrounds the entire perimeter.

"Hey, look at that," Zack says, pointing toward the fence.

You pull Ashley over to where he's crouched down inspecting the chain link. This part of the fence is sooty and black like it's been burned. The ground around it is charred. A huge padlock hangs from a chain, joining the two pieces of fencing. A singe mark trails across the front of it.

"What happened to it?" Ashley asks. Zack adjusts his glasses. "It must have been struck by lightning during that storm last night. See, the lock is cracked."

Sure enough, as you inspect it closely, you can see a large crack.

Zack lifts the charred metal, and it breaks apart in his hand.

You pick up a piece from where it crumbled to the ground. "I think Larsen's gonna need a new lock."

Zack unwinds the giant chain, and the gate swings forward on its own. "Should we go in?"

"You're going in there?" Ashley asks, her eyes filling with tears.

You squat down next to your sister. "Come on, Ashley. Don't wimp out on me."

She chews on her lip. "But people disappear in there."

"That's just a stupid story. Larsen probably made it up to keep people out," you say.

Ashley still looks terrified.

You study her face and hesitate. "We'd better wait till I ditch the shrimp. Besides, she'll tell my mom for sure."

"But they might fix it before we can come back," Zack says. "Larsen is serious about security, and I'm dying to know what he's hiding in there." Zack turns to Ashley. "You won't tell, will you?"

Ashley bites her lip but shakes her head no.

"See," Zack says. "She won't tell."

You know the chances of Ashley not telling your mom and dad are about as good as your grandma sending you something besides socks for your birthday, but you're curious about what's behind that fence too.

You take your sister's hand and step through the opening. "I promise we'll take care of you."

Zack follows and rewraps the chain, so no one will notice right away that there's anything different about the fence.

The path is more overgrown here than outside the gate, but it's still a pretty defined roadway that leads toward a heavily forested area. About twenty yards down the road, you see a large sign. It reads:

YOU ARE NOW ENTERING THE LAND OF THE GAMEKEEPER

"The Gamekeeper?" Zack asks. "Is that like a game warden?"

"Beats me," you say.

Zack glances at the trees. "Should we be worried about wild animals?"

"Around here?" you say. "I doubt there's anything bigger than a raccoon."

His eyes grow big. "Have you ever seen an angry raccoon? Cartoons lie. Those things are terrifying."

You snicker. "Don't worry, I'll protect you from any wild raccoons we come across."

There's another sign. This one reads:

LAST CHANCE! TURN BACK OR BE BOUND.

THE GAMEKEEPER

"Again, from The Gamekeeper," Zack says.

"And bound?" you wonder aloud. You read the sign again. "Are they saying they're going to tie us up if they catch us here?"

Ashley looks at you in alarm.

You squeeze her hand to reassure her.

"Usually they say they're going to take you to jail or fine you for trespassing," Zack says.

An uneasy feeling comes over you. "Mr. Larsen is pretty weird. My mom says he used to be a nice guy, but he had some kind of accident. That's why he has that bad limp and all those scars on his face."

Zack squints at the sun and looks around to get his bearing. "I heard it was a car accident."

"Maybe, but his daughter was with him. They say she disappeared. What kind of car accident does that?" you ask as you come to a smaller sign marked:

BOUNDARY LINE

"It's just a story," he says. "You worry too much." He points to the sign. "This is it. Are you still in?"

You glance at Ashley, who hasn't changed her

expression since you entered the forest. If Zack wasn't so sure of himself, you might turn back, too. There is no way you're going to chicken out now. You squeeze Ashley's hand, and you both step across the line.

Zack is right behind you.

As your foot breaks the boundary, the regular forest sounds become momentarily muted. A wave of energy pushes through you. The sun is suddenly dimmer. The wind picks up. Leaves and dirt fly through the air around you.

You cover your face with your arm and try to block Ashley with your body. Then, just as quickly as it came, the wind is gone.

When you lift your head, there's a tall hooded figure dressed all in black standing before you. He seems more pleased than shocked to see you.

"Welcome," he says with a flourish of his hand toward the forest, "to the game."

CHAPTER 2

You stare at the hooded man. "Who are you?" His pale, pointed face lifts into an unpleasant smile. "I am The Gamekeeper, and this is my land."

"Are we gonna go to jail?" Ashley whispers.

Zack holds up his hands. "We were just curious. We didn't mean to bother anyone."

You start to back up. As you get to the boundary sign, something solid stops your foot. You turn around. A high, glimmering wall stretches up in front of you. You push against it, but it's thick and solid. You're trapped.

Zack kicks at the wall. "Hey, what's this?"

The Gamekeeper lifts his hood. His black hair peaks in the middle of his forehead and hangs limply at his shoulders. "You have passed the return point. Now you are bound to me and to the game."

You take a step toward him. "What game? What are you talking about?"

"Yeah, and what do you mean by 'bound' to you?" Zack says.

The Gamekeeper looks at you both as if you were

bugs under a glass. "You're not very bright, are you?" He gives a disappointed sigh. "I suppose you'll have to do. Beggars can't be choosers, and that fool, Larsen, has kept me without anyone to play with for far too long."

Zack seems as confused as you are.

The Gamekeeper leans against a tree and picks at his nails. "I'll explain, and I'll use small words, so you're sure to understand. By passing the boundary line, you entered a contract to play my game. To get home, you must battle through my world."

Zack looks at you. "I don't think we should do it. The closest I've ever been to a battle is on my computer, and believe me, I always use the cheat codes."

"What if we don't play?" you ask.

The Gamekeeper's smug look hardens into an icy stare. "If you don't play, then you stay here forever. The only way back is to win."

"But we didn't know this was your land," you say.

The Gamekeeper looks bored as he gestures to the path. "The signs were clearly posted."

Ashley stamps her foot. "I don't want to stay

here. I want to go home right now!"

The Gamekeeper turns to her in surprise. "Finally, some spirit." His eyes light up with hungry excitement. He turns back to you and Zack, his gaze traveling over you as if sizing you up. "Since you don't look like warriors, and your chances of survival are rather small, I'll make you a deal.

I'll give you your freedom in exchange for something you'll never miss . . ." His beady eyes shift toward Ashley. ". . . your responsibility."

The Gamekeeper snaps his fingers, and the barrier and Ashley disappear from beside you.

You look around wildly. "What did you do to her?"

"Oh, relax." The Gamekeeper waves his hand as if to brush off your concern. "I've given you a gift. Now you can go back to your lives. You're free."

You shake your head. "But, what about my sister?"

I promise to care for her, perhaps even mold her into my assistant." The Gamekeeper lifts his eyebrows. "At the very least, I've been wanting another pet."

"I can't leave without her."

He puts an arm around your shoulder and his other around Zack. Everything about him is cold. Even through your shirt, his touch gives you the shivers.

His voice is almost a whisper. "Once you decide to leave, no one will remember her at all. Not you— not your parents— not even your little, spectacled friend." He turns you toward the way out. "It will be as if she never existed. You'll be free. No more whining little sister. No more babysitting."

He pushes you and Zack toward the boundary line. "All you have to do is take a step across that line, and this whole nightmare will end. Forget about the girl, and you can go home."

You look down the path toward freedom, your foot aching to take the step. Then you think of Ashley. You wonder where she is and if she's okay. You plant your feet and push away from The Gamekeeper. "I'm not leaving her!"

Zack steps behind you. "Me either."

The Gamekeeper's eyes narrow. "Fine. Have it your way." He snaps again, and the barrier reappears.

You look around for Ashley. "Where's my sister?"

The smug look is back on The Gamekeeper's face. "Oh, that." He shrugs. "I decided to keep her anyway."

"You can't do that!" Zack yells.

Anger flashes in The Gamekeeper's cruel eyes. "Oh, can't I? You're in my world now. I made you an excellent bargain. It's not my fault you're not bright enough to take it. When you're killed in this place, I'll get the girl, anyway."

"You're nothing but a cheat and a bully," you yell.

"Well." The Gamekeeper claps his hands together like a delighted child. "You do have some fight in you. This might be fun, after all." He crosses his heart with his finger. "I promise I'll keep your sister safe and send you back to your boring little lives *if* you make it through."

"With my sister?"

He looks annoyed. "Yes, yes, with your sister."

BONUS ROLL: FOR SHOWING BRAVERY BY STANDING UP TO THE GAMEKEEPER, YOU EARN A BONUS ROLL.

ROLL ONE DIE. IF YOU ROLL A 5 OR 6, YOU EARN A HEALING POTION THAT WILL ADD FIVE LIFE POINTS.

The Gamekeeper moves closer. He stares down at you and Zack. "Now, where was I? Oh yes. The rules are simple. To win, all you have to do is reach the other end of the forest. . . alive."

The reality of this game sinks in. You look over at Zack and try to swallow around the lump in your throat. "I should have let you leave when we had the chance. Ashley's *my* sister."

Zack pushes up his glasses and squares his skinny shoulders. "We've got a better chance of surviving if we do this together." He's a good friend, but you really wish he were a Navy Seal right now.

The Gamekeeper wipes away an imaginary tear. "This is all so touching, but we must get to it." He claps his hands together.

All sounds in the forest go unnaturally quiet. Fog gathers around The Gamekeeper's spindly legs. It gets thicker, surrounding him. He gives you a little half-bow. "Your game . . . starts. . . NOW!"

With a dramatic wave of his arms, the fog sweeps over him, and then he's gone. The vapor pours forward, surrounding both you and Zack. You can't see anything.

A strange rustling sound echoes through the trees.

Whoosh. . .

Whoosh. . .

Whoosh.

At first you think it's the wind, but then it gets louder.

WHhoooooosSh!

You and Zack look around, but it's so hard to see through the fog.

WHOOSH.

A crow slices through the mist, nearly hitting you. Its loud squawk echoes through the trees. Another appears and then another. The mist is thinning. You can see hundreds of birds perched in the crooked branches of the forest.

You take a step back.

The birds take flight and begin to circle.

Their calls become deafening.

One swipes at your head.

Then, another bird scratches across Zack's arm.

Without warning, they're all over both of you, diving and pecking. You're trapped in a sea of black feathers. All you can hear is the sound of wings and caw after angry caw as they dive at you.

"We have to get out of here!" you yell.

Zack covers his head with his hands.

The birds form a cyclone of claws and beaks.

You wave your arms to fight them off, but they rip at your shirt and circle again. You turn to Zack. "Run!"

The crows are relentlessly swooping down on him. You spot a large branch lying on the ground near the edge of the path. You pick it up and start to swing wildly. You feel the branch connect with hollow bird bones. The flock screeches and retreats. The crows don't go far before they turn back, ready for another attack.

THIS IS YOUR FIRST BATTLE.

ROLL THE DIE, AND MATCH THE NUMBER ON TO THE CHART. IF YOU DON"T HAVE THE BATTLE BOOK SCOREBOOK, YOU MAY WANT TO USE A BLANK PIECE OF PAPER FOR YOUR CALCULATIONS.

Roll	1	2	3	4	5	6
Crows Wounds	1	2	3	4	5	6
Your Wounds	2	1	1	0	0	0

THE CROWS START WITH FIVE LIFE POINTS. SUBTRACT THE NUMBER OF WOUNDS THEY GET ACCORDING TO THE CHART AND WRITE IT HERE

5 - ____=_______.

YOU START WITH FIFTY LIFE POINTS. NOW, SUBTRACT THE NUMBER OF WOUNDS YOU TOOK ACCORDING TO THE ROLL.

50 -_____= ______.

IF THE CROWS' POINTS REACH 0, YOU HAVE WON THIS BATTLE. IF THEY STILL HAVE POINTS LEFT, KEEP ROLLING AND SUBTRACTING UNTIL THE CROWS ARE DEFEATED. DON'T FORGET TO SUBTRACT YOUR OWN WOUND POINTS FOR EACH ROLL.

IF YOUR ROLL EARLIER EARNED YOU THE HELING POITION, ADD 5 POINTS TO YOUR SCORE. GO TO THE LAST PAGE IF YOU RUN OUT OF POINTS.

WHEN YOU DEFEAT THE CROWS, WRITE THE NUMBER OF POINTS YOU HAVE LEFT HERE ________ TO USE FOR FUTURE BATTLES.

CHAPTER 3

The birds have taken a beating. Some of them fly off through the trees, screeching protests as they go. You and Zack swing your makeshift clubs until the last of the crows flap away. The forest is quiet once again. Feathers litter the ground.

You stand back-to-back, sticks ready, unsure if the crows have gone for good. After a few minutes, you lower your weapons and look at each other. Zack's forehead is bleeding. There are holes in his shirt and talon marks across his arms and neck. Looking down, you see similar holes in your own clothing and wounds on your arms.

You expect Zack to be in shock. You doubt he's ever been in a real fight in his life. Instead, he looks happy.

"That was—amazing!" he yells. "Those crows were crazy." He swings his stick around and makes sound effects. "I was like, *bam.* Then you gave them a, *ka-pow.*" He makes a few more acrobatic swings with sound effects. "We kicked their feathery butts."

His enthusiasm is contagious, but you're worried about what else is coming for you. "We got lucky."

"Lucky?" Zack shakes his head. "We were like ninjas on steroids. Admit it. You were impressed I had some moves."

You look over at your lanky, bleeding friend. He still grips his stick like a lifeline. "You're definitely tougher than you look."

He flexes a scrawny arm and laughs. "Good thing, or we'd be in real trouble."

You take off your backpack. There are several holes in it, but it's still usable. "We need to check our supplies. Then we can form a plan."

Zack takes off his own backpack. One of the straps has been badly frayed by the birds. It's not going to hold much anymore.

Together you take inventory of your supplies: two sandwiches, a package of cookies, a couple of pairs of swim goggles, a package of beef jerky, two towels, a tee-shirt, a pair of pants for each of you, and two sweatshirts (one of which is pink and Ashley's size).

You decide to change into the pants to protect your legs. When you pull yours out, you remember your scout knife is in the pocket. You take it out, open it, and start to sharpen one end of your stick into a spear-like point.

Zack watches the curls of wood fall to the ground. "It's like making hotdog sticks."

"Only we're the ones who might end up as dinner," you say.

Zack's stomach growls. "Speaking of dinner, I'm starving."

This isn't surprising. Zack is always hungry. How a person can eat so much and still look like a skeleton is a mystery.

You look up from your sharpening. "We can split one of the sandwiches for now, but we have to conserve the food. We don't know how long we're going to be stuck in here."

"Yes!" Zack unwraps one of the sandwiches and tears it in two. He puts the plastic wrap back into the pack. "You never know what you're going to need in this place." He eats his half in record time and then takes over sharpening while you eat yours.

Zack reaches down for his canteen. It isn't there. It must have fallen from his neck during the battle.

After looking for a minute or two, you see it about ten yards away on the path. The strap is ripped, and the lid is off.

Zack retrieves it and tips it up to see if there is any water left. Only a few drops roll onto his outstretched tongue.

"We're going to have to find water soon," you say.

He looks at the sun to orient himself and then points to the left. "I think that way is west. We were headed to the lake. If I'm right, it would have been this direction." He points the opposite way toward a clump of trees. "The lake is river-fed, so if we head that way, we should run into water at some point."

You decide that plan is as good as any. Using the knife, Zack cuts long pieces from a rainbow-striped beach towel. You both attach pieces of the towel around your arms, legs, and necks, using strips cut from the extra tee-shirt. It isn't much for armor, but it's better than bare skin.

Zack snorts. "Oh yeah. Now we look

threatening." He takes a superhero stance and says in his best announcer's voice, "Rainbow boy and towel kid—on a mission to protect the world from evil."

"Could have been worse," you say. "It could have been a pink towel."

"With unicorns," Zack adds, and you both laugh.

He may not be much of a warrior, but you're glad Zack decided to stay. It makes this whole mess seem a little less horrible.

You put the jerky, Ashley's sweatshirt, and the other sandwich in Zack's backpack and everything else in your own. Then you head for the river. After walking for about twenty minutes, you hear rushing water.

You push through a tangle of thick bushes and find yourself on a sandbar next to the surging stream. The beach is full of gray and pink rocks of varying sizes. The strange stones give the beach an alien feel. The river is too swift to cross, but a little eddy provides the perfect place to get water.

Zack bends to fill the canteen, and you look around. Across the river there are more trees. There is no sign of the fence or the golden boundary. "Do you have any idea where we are?"

"Of course I do. That's easy." He pauses for effect and passes you the canteen. "We're lost."

You shake your head and take a long drink of cool water. Out of the corner of your eye, you see something shift to your right. You quickly turn toward it.

Nothing seems to be out of order, but you swear you saw something move.

In front of you, the beach stirs, and you hear a sound like two rocks knocking together. "Did you see something?"

Zack shakes his head, but then the sound echoes through the air again, this time louder. The beach is suddenly alive with the motion of rolling rocks. It sounds like a small landslide.

Zack jumps up and retrieves his stick.

You drop the canteen. Both of you watch with hearts pounding and weapons ready.

In front of you, one of the rocks splits open.

What you had thought were river rocks are little lizard-like creatures with hard, stony plates down their backs. Dozens of them have unrolled now, revealing stumpy legs, long tails, and beady red eyes. They hiss at you and flick thin, purplish tongues in and out of fanged jaws.

One starts to get close to Zack. He smacks it with his stick. With a crack like a hit to a baseball, it flies into the river.

You both back toward the tree line.

"What are those things?" you ask.

Zack readies his club again. "I don't know, but they're looking at me the way I look at a turkey sandwich."

The rock lizards are gathering into a swarm. It's like being in the middle of a hornet's nest, only these creatures are much bigger and loaded with needle-like teeth. They press toward you. One lunges at your ankle, and you stab it with the sharpened end of your stick. It lets out a shrill squeal and rolls back into a ball. The sound seems to agitate the rest.

You and Zack swing your sticks like hockey players protecting the goal. Little lizards are sent flying into the water and the rocky bank.

One bites the toe of Zack's shoe. He shakes his foot to get it off, but the fangs are sunk deep into the rubber. A hard kick sends the small beast crashing against a huddle of rock lizards. They pounce and tear it apart with their sharp fangs and claws.

Black blood oozes onto the ground. The little lizards become frenzied by the gore. They surge forward at you in a swarm of teeth and claws.

With no more room to back up, you and Zack will have to fight harder.

THIS IS YOUR SECOND BATTLE.

ROLL THE DIE. MATCH THE NUMBER ON THE DIE TO THE CHART.

Roll	1	2	3	4	5	6
Lizards Wounds	1	1	2	3	5	6
Your Wounds	2	2	1	1	1	0

THE ROCK LIZARDS START WITH 6 LIFE POINTS. SUBTRACT THE NUMBER OF WOUNDS THEY GET ACCORDING TO THE CHART AND WRITE IT HERE.

6 - ____=_______.

TRANSFER YOUR LIFE POINTS FROM THE LAST BATTLE PAGE ____.

SUBTRACT THE NUMBER OF WOUNDS YOU TAKE ACCORDING TO THE ROLL AND WRITE IT HERE. (TRANSFERRED POINTS - WOUNDS= NEW LIFE POINTS)

_______ -_____=_____.

IF THE LIZARDS' POINTS REACH 0, YOU HAVE WON THIS BATTLE. IF THEY STILL HAVE POINTS LEFT, KEEP ROLLING AND SUBTRACTING UNTIL THE LIZARDS ARE DEFEATED. DON'T FORGET TO SUBTRACT YOUR OWN WOUND POINTS FOR EACH ROLL.

GO TO THE LAST PAGE IF YOU RUN OUT OF POINTS.

WHEN YOU DEFEAT THE LIZARDS, WRITE THE NUMBER OF POINTS YOU HAVE LEFT HERE _______ TO USE FOR FUTURE BATTLES.

CHAPTER 4

You've beaten back the lizards. Those that aren't dead have splashed into the river or run toward the bushes to hide.

Zack wipes the sweat from his forehead. He pulls a long fang out of his shoe and examines it. "That's a parting gift I never expected to take home today." He puts the tooth into his pocket. "What were those things, anyway?"

You shake your head. "I don't know. I've never seen anything like them."

"Something tells me we're not in Kansas anymore, Dorothy," Zack says.

"What are you talking about?"

He turns one of the dead lizards over with his stick. "Haven't you ever seen the *Wizard of Oz*? This is not a normal forest. I don't even think we're even in our world anymore."

The Gamekeeper surprises you by materializing on the beach. "That's a very interesting observation." He stalks toward you. "Your little friend is correct. You're in my world now. Are you having fun?"

You snort. “Yeah. It’s a real blast.”

He studies the lizard bodies scattered across the beach oozing black blood among the pebbles. “This is quite impressive. Thunder lizards can be rather nasty. Especially against such. . .” He gestures toward your rainbow towel armor. “. . . primitive defenses.”

Zack glances down at the tattered material around his shins, and his cheeks blaze.

Seeing your friend humiliated by this horrible man ignites something deep in your chest. You narrow your eyes. “You’ll have to excuse us for leaving our chainmail at home, but we didn’t exactly get a packing list.”

The Gamekeeper points at you. “See, that’s exactly the kind of spirit that makes me think you might make it through. You’ve got fight in you. It’s buried under layers of fast food and soft living, but it’s in there.”

You ignore his predictions. “Where’s my sister?”

He rubs his spindly fingers absently over his chin. “She’s fine. She’s being cared for by one of my. . . associates.” Something about the way he says *associates* makes your skin crawl.

"You better not hurt her."

He chuckles. "My current plans are for her absolute safety, but if I change my mind, I promise you'll be the first to know."

You can't stand the thought of Ashley at his mercy. "If you hurt her, I swear I'll make you sorry."

The Gamekeeper paces a few steps away. When he looks back at you, fury dances in his eyes. "*You'll* make *me* sorry? Clearly, you don't seem to understand the situation, so I'll enlighten you."

The dark man puts his hands out in front of him. As he turns them, the whole beach begins to tip. You and Zack struggle to stay upright as rocks and the water in the riverbed slide sideways. The Gamekeeper is the only thing unaffected by the tilt. At the same time, the once clear sky boils with black, swirling clouds.

The Gamekeeper stands like a dark pillar in the middle of slashing lightning and twisting darkness. "As your pasty friend here so cleverly put it, you are not in Kansas anymore, boy. This is my world. I make the rules here."

He gradually increases the incline so that you and

Zack are sliding along with the smaller rocks toward what is now a steep drop-off. You grab for anything solid to keep yourselves from the edge.

It's obvious The Gamekeeper is enjoying your fear. "Now, while I find your fighting spirit amusing in my little game, our lack of respect needs to be remedied, one way or the other." The beach is nearly vertical now, leaving you and Zack clinging to one of the larger boulders, your feet dangling above a dangerous fall.

He looks at you. "Do we have an understanding?"

You want to argue, but Zack's fingers are starting to slip, so you nod your head yes. The Gamekeeper releases his hands, and the world rights. The water sloshes back to its place in the riverbed. The sky clears. You and Zack are lying on the beach, your arms still wrapped around the boulders. Realizing that the world is flat again, you stand and help Zack up.

The Gamekeeper adjusts his long black cloak. "Now, where were we? Oh yes, your sister." His eyes light up with genuine delight.

"She's an absolute terror, and that amuses me.

She actually bit one of my trolls. I've grown rather fond of her. So, I've come to make you another deal."

"Did he say Ashley bit a troll?" Zack whispers.

You nod your head and wait as The Gamekeeper removes a pair of black gloves from his cloak and slides them over his thin fingers.

He gestures toward you.

A chest of gold coins and jewels appears at your feet. "I'm upping my ante," he says. "You can take this chest and return to your families right now. No more battles. All you have to do is say I get the girl. I'll snap my fingers and send you and the chest right to your cozy little doorstep. Do we have a deal?"

You hang your head. You'd love to go home, but you can't leave Ashley. "I'm not leaving without my sister."

The Gamekeeper continues as if you hadn't spoken. "It's a very generous offer. I doubt any of the creatures in this forest will give you such a deal."

Zack pushes his glasses forcefully onto his nose. "He said we aren't interested."

The Gamekeeper is smiling, but he grits his teeth. "Ever the little heroes. Well, rules are rules.

I guess I'll just have to wait till something finishes you off, but you should know it's only going to get worse from here on out. Lizards and crows are nothing. Wait till you meet the rest of my creatures."

"We can't leave without my sister!" you yell, your frustration outweighing your fear of the cruel man.

The Gamekeeper wags a pointed finger. "Temper, temper. Didn't anyone ever tell you games are supposed to be fun?"

"Fun?" Zack says. "Fun? You trapped us in this forest to fight until we die. How is that fun?"

The pale man raises his thin eyebrows. "Ah, but you see. That is fun. . . for me." With the flap of his cloak, The Gamekeeper disappears again, leaving you and Zack alone on the beach.

After a few minutes in silence, you decide to act. You tighten the pieces of the towel around your shins. "I'm going to go get the canteen. The sooner we find Ashley, the sooner this nightmare can end." You walk over to the river, retrieving the battered water bottle.

It's only half full, so you take it to the water's edge to fill it the rest of the way. You'd rather just get out of here, but you don't know when your next chance to get water will be. You keep a sharp look out for any signs that the lizards are coming back.

Deep inside, you fight the panic rising in your chest. The Gamekeeper was right. You aren't a warrior. Zack is great, but you're in trouble here. You need some real help. A strange feeling pulses through you. Your knees buckle slightly, and you struggle to stand. Just as quickly as it comes over you, it's gone. You're a little light headed, but you don't have time to dwell on it.

You turn toward the tree line where Zack is standing. "I think we should. . ."

Behind him, in the trees, is a huge white wolf the size of a horse.

"Zack." You try to keep your voice calm. "Walk toward me, very slowly. Don't turn around."

Zack cringes but eases himself your way. "It's a giant spider, isn't it? There's *always* a giant spider. Don't let it suck out my blood, okay?"

"It's not a giant spider," you say. "Just keep walking."

He looks relieved. Then he glances over his

shoulder and catches sight of the wolf.

His eyes grow big, and he gives a little whimper. "Oh yeah, that's much better. Now all I can think of is that I look like a big can of dog food." He tries to stay calm and walk slowly, but he ends up sort of power-walking toward you.

The wolf stands motionless and silent, watching you.

"At least he seems friendly," Zack says.

You look at him like he's crazy. "Friendly?" "Well, he's not growling or snarling."

"So now you're the dog whisperer? That isn't exactly a poodle. Aggressive or not, we're out of here."

You back toward the river.

Zack looks indignant. "I wasn't saying we should try to pet it. I just—" His focus shifts to something behind you, and his face pales. He shoves you to the ground and then leaps to his right.

A large object smashes into the ground beside you. At first you think it's a giant harpoon, but it's attached to something under the water like an octopus arm. You scramble backward, crab-style, to get away. Zack stumbles down the beach.

A creature, the color of melted silver, crawls out of the water. It pulls itself along the beach toward you with two muscular gray arms. Four three-inch claws, the color of tar, protrude from each powerful arm. They slash easily through the packed sand and rock. You can only imagine what they could do to you.

What you thought was a harpoon is actually a sharp-tipped tail, hovering in the air ready to strike again. The animal looks like a giant scorpion but with a flat, silver body and a huge mouth full of long teeth. A sound like a saw blade scraping along iron screeches from its gaping jaws.

Zack runs back toward you and tries to keep the monstrosity away with his stick. As it pulls itself further from the water, the creature doesn't appear to have any back legs. It uses the sharp tail and arms to creep toward you, dragging its legless backside along the ground.

You jump to your feet and start to run.

The creature lets out another wail. The tail comes down again, spearing your backpack and pinning you to the ground. You're trapped.

With his tail spearing the pack, you can't get the tight straps off your shoulders.

The river creature drags itself forward. Its huge mouth slurps and drools as it claws toward you, hungry for a meal. It's right on top of you. Zack hits it with the stick. It shrieks at him with another metallic screech. The sound makes your ears ring.

It grabs at Zack but doesn't release the backpack. You can't get away. Zack has to back off to avoid the creature's slashing claws. It turns its focus on you. Slowly its jagged mouth lowers. There's no escape. You close your eyes and wait for the needle-sharp teeth to sink into your skin.

Through the commotion, you hear something crash out of the trees and thunder across the beach toward you. You see white fur just as the wolf's massive jaws pierce the hard shell of the scorpion's body. The creature lifts its tail, and you're suddenly free.

With one shake of his enormous head, the wolf flings the scorpion creature in a wide arc. It hits the beach ten feet away and skids to a stop on its back, exposing a flat-shelled underbelly. The dangerous tail swings around like a bullwhip through the air.

You struggle to your feet, and both you and Zack run toward the trees. As you look back, the wolf crouches between you and the river creature. The fur on its body stands rigid. He bares his enormous teeth and growls savagely at the scorpion.

Zack, panting from his run, nods toward the creature. "See, now that's aggressive behavior."

You look at Zack in amazement.

Sinking its tail into the rocky beach for leverage, the river monster uses its clawed arms to right itself. It advances, bringing the spear tail down close to the wolf's shoulder. The snarling canine snaps at the tail and then backs up. He repeats the pattern, rushing in to bite at the animal then retreating from the threat of claws, teeth, and tail.

The creature claws at the wolf and brings the spear tail down again, narrowly missing the animal's head. It smashes deep into the rocks and sand. The white muzzle surges forward. His teeth grip deep into sinew and shell. He shakes fiercely.

The shelled creature's arm dangles, useless, from its torso as it's flung, once again, to the earth.

"Go wolf-man." Zack cheers.

"How do you know that the river scorpion isn't just the appetizer? We don't know anything about that wolf. He might just be mad that thing interrupted his dinner plans."

Zack stands firm. "He saved your life. I'm not saying I want to name him Fluffy, but I'm rooting for the wolf."

The lethal tail whips through the air. This time it hits the wolf squarely in the side. The blow sends him tumbling across the beach. The wolf seems dazed and struggles to get his feet under him. The scorpion advances. Its tail arches, ready to deliver a deadly blow to the wolf.

Zack pelts the river monster with rocks. "We have to help him."

You're not sure it's a wise decision, but you join in, throwing rocks and yelling until the creature turns its attention to you.

It roars a metallic warning and slashes its claws through the air. With renewed strength, the wolf recovers and pushes itself onto his feet. Snarling and barking, the wolf rejoins the fight. The scorpion shrieks continually, his attention torn between the two enemies.

With a mighty lunge, the wolf latches onto the creature's tail with vice-like jaws. He continues to shake it until the creature's body hangs limp and immobile.

You nudge Zack and retreat for the trees before the wolf turns his attention toward you. Slipping through the bushes near the river, you push through the undergrowth until you see the main path, where you fought the crows. At least for now, you're out of immediate danger.

Zack shakes his head. "Who knew we'd be happy to see this place again?"

"Well, there isn't a giant animal about to eat us here." You look around cautiously. "At least not one we can see."

Zack has an excited half–grin on his face. "You have to admit that wolf was pretty cool, though. He was like a supersized attack dog. I wish we could have taken a picture of him or something."

Before you can answer, the sound of breaking sticks catches your attention. The wolf jumps through a gap in the bushes to land squarely in front of you.

"Hey, Zack," you say through trembling lips, "still want that picture?"

CHAPTER 5

The wolf stands on the road in front of you. At this range, you can see that your head only reaches his shoulder. His paws are the size of dinner plates. Yellow eyes search your faces as he swivels his massive, shaggy head from you to Zack and back again.

You talk softly over your shoulder to Zack, unwilling to look away from the wolf. "I told you we should have run when we had the chance, but oh no, we have to help the wolf. Still think he's the one who needs protecting?"

Zack's voice waivers, "Do you really need me to agree with you? I promise, if we live through this, you can make all future decisions involving huge, mutant dogs."

The wolf circles the two of you cautiously. He tilts his head as if trying to figure something out. He steps close to Zack and sniffs him. Zack's legs are shaking, and his eyes are squeezed shut.

The wolf sneezes and shakes his head. He circles around to you, tentatively taking in your scent. His furry body presses against you as his hot breath tickles at your neck and head.

With a whine, the wolf steps back. He stands next to you, panting heavily. He whimpers again and then walks down the path. When you don't follow, he turns back to you as if he's waiting.

You and Zack are statues on the road. The wolf pads back, this time nudging you forward with his huge head. You take a few steps, then stop and look back at the wolf. He tilts his head again, as if to say, "What's your problem?" Then he nudges you again and repeats the same process with Zack, herding you both forward.

"I think he wants us to go with him," you say.

As you take a few cautious steps down the path, the wolf seems convinced you understand and resumes the lead. He looks back often, probably to make sure that you're both still following.

Zack breaks the silence. "Do you know where a five-hundred-pound wolf leads two boys in the woods?" Without waiting for you to answer, he finishes. "Anywhere he wants." Leave it to Zack to crack a joke at a time like this.

After following the main road for ten minutes, the wolf stops at what looks like a deer trail that splits off to the left. He waits. When you and Zack are close enough, he turns down the path.

You shrug at Zack and push through some tall grass to follow. The trail winds through a variety of itchy weeds, trees, and strange plants until you come to a cliff face towering above you. You look up at the tall mountain. The wolf continues to lead you along a winding path that hugs the base of the mountain.

After a short time, you come to a narrow cave opening. It looks like a jagged mouth cut out of the mountain. The wolf stands in front of the opening. He whines softly and then gives a loud bark.

"I guess he wants us to go in," Zack says.

You nod. "I know. I'm just wondering if he's helping us or bringing home take-out for his family."

The wolf nudges you again.

Zack takes off his glasses and cleans them on his shirt. "You do sort of look like a Big Mac, but I don't think we have much of a choice."

Zack's right. You take a deep breath and step into the uncertainty of the cave's dark entrance.

Because of the size of the opening, you expected the cavern to be small, but it's nearly ten feet tall on the inside. An unusual yellow glow emanates from the back of the cave.

"Whoa," Zack says, stepping into the cave behind you. "What's making that light?"

You try to peer ahead, but a large outcropping of rocks partially blocks your view.

You hear the wolf moving behind you and turn to see him push through the narrow entrance. His huge furry body barely fits. Walking past you, he takes the lead again and heads toward the dusky yellow light.

You fall in behind him. "I guess we're about to find out."

The cave smells damp and earthy but pleasant. In the distance, a steady drip of water echoes off the rocks.

As you round the outcrop, you can see that the glow comes from a gem the size of your head. It sits at eye level, half-buried in the cave wall. In a small cache below the jewel is a pile of weapons. A variety of axes with wicked-looking blades and huge metal swords are stacked in the small depression.

You step closer and examine them. Each is unique but beautifully designed. Some of them glow red like they have a living fire inside. Some are blue and covered in frost. One strange sword sizzles and sparks as you move it slightly with your foot.

Zack peers over your shoulder. "Those definitely beat our sticks. This place is like the bat cave."

"Should we just take one?" You turn to look to the wolf for direction, but he's gone. "Where's the wolf?"

"What do you mean, 'Where's the wolf?'" Zack says, scanning the area, "He was right in front of us. I'm not the most observant guy in the world, but I think I would have noticed a six-foot wolf squeeze past me."

You look around. "He's gone."

Zack appears resigned. "Normally I'd freak out, but after everything else that's happened today, I'm just going with it."

"He led us here for a reason," you say. "I guess we're supposed to take a weapon."

Zack's eyes sparkle with the reflection of the

jewel's glow. "Again, can I just say that wolf is awesome?"

As you reach toward the weapons, your hand starts to buzz. The vibrations flow up your arm. Somehow, you're sure you'll know which weapon is destined to be yours. You close your eyes and let the magic take over as you reach toward the cache.

ZACK ALREADY PICKED AN AXE. NOW IT'S YOUR TURN TO CHOOSE. ROLL THE DIE TO DETERMINE WHICH TYPE OF SWORD YOU WILL USE THROUGHOUT THE GAME.

Roll	1	2	3	4	5	6
	Frost Sword	Lightning Sword	Shadow Sword	Fire Sword	Time Sword	Elemental Sword

CHAPTER 6

This whole day seems like a dream. Only a few hours ago, you were eating waffles in your kitchen. Now you're brandishing a sword in a hidden cave. Normally you'd think it was really cool, but that was before everything in this world started trying to kill you.

You walk back to where Zack crouches in the cache. He stands and swings a long-handled, two-bladed axe that has a faint blue glow to it. When he moves it, it crackles like it's charged with energy. "Hey, look at this," he says, placing his axe carefully on the ground outside the small space. "There's something else under here."

He pushes swords and axes to the side. Beneath the weapons are several pieces of armor. They appear to be made of different metals and vary in design. As you examine the shape of them and where the leather straps are placed, you realize they're chest plates.

Zack pulls out the nearest plate. He knocks his hand against the metal. "He got us some armor, too? Man, I love that wolf."

You snort. "Yeah, now we might survive at least one night in this place."

Each chest plate is slightly different with various symbols of different animals cast into the metal. Zack takes a copper colored one with the head of a howling wolf on the front of it. He searches through a few more and hands you one with a silver wolf's paw print and face enclosed in a golden circle.

You raise your eyebrows at the wolf symbol.

Zack pushes it toward you forcefully. "This way he'll know we're on the same side."

You shake your head, but as you take the armor, the same type of tingling you felt from the sword runs up your arm, convincing you this armor is supposed to be yours.

After putting on the armor, you look around the cave. It's not that big, but it feels safe. You're tempted to stay here, but you've got to get to Ashley.

The sunlight hurts your eyes as you step back through the cave opening and breathe in the piney tang of the forest. The sword feels heavy and clumsy in your hand, and the new chest plate rubs slightly at the shoulder straps.

Zack follows you out of the cave, awkwardly dragging his axe. He turns it over, so the handle is resting on the ground. He studies the wicked curves of the metal, testing the sharpness by rubbing a thumb gently across the blades. The sun glints off the wolf emblazoned across his chest.

You have to admit he looks a little more like a warrior now even with leg and arm bracers made of a rainbow towel.

Zack shields his eyes and scans the forest. "Still no wolf? I wonder where he went."

You'd also hoped the wolf would be waiting outside the cave. Only twisted trees and dense shrubs lie in front of you, and the rugged face of the cliff towers at your back. "Maybe he has more important things to do than babysit us."

Disappointment clouds Zack's features.

You nudge his shoulder. "Come on. You've read all those Clifford books. Huge dogs lead very busy lives, but they always save the day."

Zack opens his mouth to offer a comeback, but he's interrupted by the sound of a feminine voice. "You ran out of valor tokens."

Both you and Zack jump and turn toward the sound. A girl, close to your own age, with braided red hair and an assault of freckles across her face stands on the other side of the path, partially hidden by the nearest tree. You swear you just looked over there when you were searching for the wolf. Where did she come from?

"Apparently," Zack says under his breath, "in this world, no one enters a space normally. Appear. Disappear. It's all they do."

You elbow him in the ribs to quiet him.

She steps out from behind the tree. "My name is Kayla. I didn't mean to scare you."

Zack puffs out his chest. "We weren't scared. Maybe surprised . . . jumpy, I guess." He looks to you for back up. "Yeah, we're jumpy. . . from all the fighting." He tries to lift the axe but ends up fumbling it. It clatters to the ground. His cheeks flame. "We were just alert. Yeah, I'd say it was an alertness rather than fear. . ."

You have no idea how to help him. Talking to girls has never been his strong suit, but this is worse than usual. "Please stop talking,"

He nods his head. "Good idea."

A small smile escapes the girl's lips, but she doesn't address his awkwardness. "I was just saying that the wolf is gone because you ran out of valor tokens." She seems to note the confused looks on both of your faces. "You've never heard of valor tokens? Wow, you must be really new."

You look closely at her. She's dressed like a warrior in a full set of leather armor, but underneath, she has on a button-up shirt and jeans, leading you to believe that she hasn't always been part of this world.

"Valor tokens are what you earn with each battle," the girl continues. "The bigger the win, the more valor tokens you earn. You can't summon your Guardian until you've gained enough." She walks over and gently takes your sword. She flips it over and points to a smooth blue stone on the hilt. "This is your valor stone. When it glows, you know you've earned enough points to summon your Guardian. If you came in together, your stones are connected."

"So that huge wolf really is here for us— like a helper or something?" you ask.

"Guardian," she corrects.

You roll the word around in your mouth trying to get used to it. "Guardian."

Zack interrupts. "Told you he was awesome." He picks up his axe and finds his own valor stone on the bottom of the handle. "Say hello to team wolfman." He holds his hand up to you for a high five.

"I don't understand," you say, ignoring Zack's hand, looking instead toward the girl. "You said we had to summon him."

"Yes."

"But he came to us before, and we didn't summon anything."

The girl thinks for a moment. "Were you about to get your butts kicked?"

Zack starts to explain, but you silence him with a gesture and nod yes.

"Then whether you know it or not, you summoned him."

A loud screech from above makes Zack duck and then cover his head.

Kayla holds out her arm. "It's only Ismael, my Guardian," she says with a chuckle. A small hawk circles around your heads and lands softly on the leather bracer around her arm.

"Relax already," you say to Zack. "Your 'alertness' is starting to get embarrassing."

The sharp talons grip the protective leather as Kayla leans her head against the bird affectionately. It appears to be an average-looking hawk although his feathers have a strange metallic look to them.

"That's your Guardian?" Zack asks.

The girl nods.

He squints his eyes. "Kind of small, isn't he?"

"He's precisely the size needed to protect me." She glares at Zack. "Besides, looks can be deceiving." She raises her arm and makes a clicking sound. Ismael lifts from his perch and begins to circle in the sky.

You have a hard time keeping track of his quick movements through the trees. You catch sight of him to your right, flying like lightning toward one of the biggest trees.

For a moment you think he'll crash into it. Right before the tree, he starts to spin like a corkscrew, still barreling toward the mighty trunk. More quickly than you can follow with your eye, he's out the other side, and there is a large hole all the way through the gigantic tree.

He flies back up, circles the sky with another majestic screech, and alights on Kayla's outstretched arm once again.

She pets his head and croons to him softly. Looking pointedly at Zack, she says, "The size of one's Guardian doesn't determine the fight in them."

"I guess not. That was amazing." He steps in for a closer look and speaks softly to the bird. The girl's face softens. She has just learned something you found out long ago. There is no use being mad at Zack. He puts his foot in his mouth most days, but he has a contagious enthusiasm that makes it nearly impossible to stay angry with him.

Kayla is smiling now as she talks with Zack.

With her features softened, she looks less like a warrior and more like any ordinary girl. You wonder how long she's been in this forest and if there are others like her. "I hope it didn't use too many of your valor tokens to call Ismael for us."

The girl's smile melts from her lips, and her eyes drop to the ground. "I no longer require valor tokens to call Ismael. I am out of the game."

It takes a few moments for this statement to register.

Of course Zack is the first to speak. "You mean you're . . .?" He can't seem to find the right word.

Kayla rescues him. "Just another part of this world now. I got attacked by a fiery cat creature with three eyes." She looks at her shoes. "I tried to fight it, but it was too strong. Now I'm stuck here forever."

You search for something to say, but the words are stuck in your throat. You try to mutter an apology, but the girl holds up a hand to silence you.

"Quiet," She commands. "Listen."

You strain your ears, and then you hear it. A faint rumbling sound, like a distant earthquake, echoes through the trees. None of you talk, each listening for the sound. It's getting louder now.

Kayla releases Ismael into the sky. "I need to see," she says to him. Her eyes change to the same blue as your valor stone. "Ismael also gives me the gift of sight. I can see what he sees."

Zack's jaw drops. "You mean you can look through Ismael's eyes?"

Kayla nods. Ismael's warning cries echo against the cliff face. "Blood grubs," Kayla says, her eyes returning to normal. "They're nearly here."

The ground beneath your feet begins to vibrate. Kayla seems to be fading in front of your eyes. You can practically see through her.

"Wait. Don't go." Zack pleads.

She shakes her head. "I can't help it. Using Ismael's powers took more out of me than I thought." She is steadily fading away. She grabs Zack's arm. "If you survive this battle, follow the path along the cliff. It will lead you to another cave. It's safe there." Before she disappears completely, she calls out. "Ready your weapons! They're here."

You stand back to back with Zack, feeling the earth rumble under your feet. You grip your sword, and Zack lifts his axe, resting its weight on his shoulder. The blades glow again with a faint blue light. They don't feel heavy anymore. You think it's strange, but you don't have time to question it.

About ten feet away, the ground bursts open, and a huge, black worm lifts its body into the light. It's nearly twelve feet tall at full height with a gaping mouth full of several circles of teeth and two large, pincer-like tusks. The ground is erupting all around, exposing at least ten more of them. They make growling sounds.

"Since when do worms have teeth?" Zack says.

"Everything here has teeth."

The first worm crawls toward you, pincers flailing. You swing your sword. As the metal sweeps through the air, you feel power surge up your arm. You spin and bring the sword down with a slicing motion, cutting the worm in two.

Zack's jaw drops open. "When did you learn to do that?"

"I'm not sure." You're just as surprised as he is. Your body seems to know what to do. You turn and slice the head off another worm. "It has something to do with this armor, I think."

Zack swipes his axe through the air like a baseball bat, removing the head from a worm in the process.

Your arms burst with strength, and the once heavy sword now feels like plastic in your hand. "The armor must be enchanted to help us fight."

"Duck," Zack yells. His axe flies over your head

with a whooshing sound. It hits a worm behind you, cleaving it in two before sticking into the side of the mountain.

"You could have killed me."

Zack pulls his axe from the rock and grins. "Enchanted armor, remember?"

Thick slime oozes down the side of your head and drips onto your shoulder. Looking up, you see one of the worms towering above you. The ground vibrates as more grubs erupt all around you. You tighten your grip on your sword. With a nod to Zack, you continue to fight for your lives.

ARE YOUR READY TO FIGHT?

ROLL ONE DIE. IF YOU HAVE THE LIGHTNING SWORD OR THE TIME SWORD, DOUBLE THE WOUNDS TO THE WORMS WITH EACH HIT ON A ROLL OF 1, 3, OR 5.

IF YOU HAVE THE SHADOW SWORD, TAKE NO WOUNDS ON A ROLL OF 1 OR 6.

Roll	1	2	3	4	5	6
Blood Grubs' Wounds	1	2	3	4	5	6
Your Wounds	2	2	1	1	1	0

THE GRUBS START WITH TEN LIFE POINTS. SUBTRACT THE NUMBER OF WOUNDS THEY GOT ACCORDING TO THE CHART AND WRITE IT HERE. 10 - ____=_______.

TRANSFER YOUR LIFE POINTS FROM THE LAST BATTLE PAGE ____. SUBTRACT THE NUMBER OF WOUNDS YOU TOOK ACCORDING TO THE ROLL AND WRITE IT HERE. (TRANSFERRED POINTS – WOUNDS = NEW LIFE POINTS) _______ -_____= ______.

IF THE GRUBS' POINTS REACH 0, YOU HAVE WON THIS BATTLE. KEEP ROLLING AND SUBTRACTING UNTIL THE GRUBS ARE DEFEATED. DON'T FORGET TO SUBTRACT YOUR OWN WOUND POINTS FOR EACH ROLL.

GO TO THE LAST PAGE IF YOU RUN OUT OF POINTS. WRITE THE NUMBER OF POINTS YOU HAVE LEFT HERE _______.

CHAPTER 7

You've got a few new bumps and scrapes from the battle with the blood grubs, but you're alive. Knowing about the Guardians and that there might be others here in the game who can help you gives you hope. You and Zack walk along the bottom of the cliff, following the path Kayla told you about.

Birds and insects call out through the trees as you travel. You take this as a sign that everything is safe since the smaller creatures seem to disappear when danger is close. After nearly an hour of walking, the path winds away from the cliff face and back into the trees.

"Are you sure we should follow it?" Zack asks. "I don't like wondering what's hiding in the trees."

"Well, we've been attacked in the trees, on the beach, and next to the cliff. I don't think it matters whether we're in the forest or not."

A hawk's cry from above draws your attention. You see the metallic glint against the sun. "It's Ismael," you say. "Kayla must be close."

A funny grin spreads over Zack's face. He pushes

past you, quickening his pace.

You grab his arm. "Hold up, Romeo. We still need to be careful."

"Who says I'm not being careful?" He shakes you off and keeps walking. "I wonder if she saw how awesome we were against those worm things."

You see a large shadow in the trees. "Zack, wait."

"No way. I'm going first. I need to look like the leader. Girls like a man that . . ."

"Zack!"

He stops walking and looks back at you with irritation. "What?"

You can only point as the shadow lumbers forward and solidifies into a huge bear blocking the path not six feet from you.

Zack sees the bear and puts a hand on his axe. "What. . . what do we do?"

You stare, wide eyed. "Do I look like a forest ranger?"

"I think I read somewhere that you're supposed to make yourself look taller than the bear, and they'll walk away," Zack says, but his voice lacks confidence.

You take in the size of the bear. "Good luck.

We'd need a truck to be bigger than that thing."

Zack slowly pulls his axe from the scabbard on his back. "Here goes nothing." He raises it above his head. "AAAAAAGHHH. Shoo, bear."

The bear looks at him with bored curiosity. It chuffs a couple of times and then rises onto its hind legs and roars. The sound is deafening and terrifying.

Kayla's voice surprises you from behind. "You boys really know how to make friends."

Zack puts a hand up. "Stay back, Kayla. I think we made it mad."

"Oh, I'd say that is more than accurate." She walks past you, heading straight for the bear. "What's the matter, Goliath? Are these nasty boys ruining your breakfast?"

The bear drops to the ground, and Kayla pulls a bunch of grapes out of her pack and gives them to the bear. As it eats, she rubs her hands against its neck. Goliath makes a series of low throaty sounds as she scratches its back and haunches. "Did those bad boys scare you?"

"Yeah," you say, pointing to the enormous bear. "That's how it happened. *We* scared *him*, nearly frightened the little guy to death. Look at him. He's a monster."

Kayla pulls out more grapes. "Is that any way to talk about a Guardian?"

Zack finally lowers his axe. "You have another Guardian?"

A man who appears to be in his late twenties steps through the trees behind the bear. "Goliath is mine." He gestures to Kayla. "He does have a soft spot for this one, though, probably because she's always feeding him."

"This is John," Kayla explains.

You acknowledge him with a nod. A short beard that matches the inky color of his hair covers his face. He has on a chest plate and arm and leg protectors made of a strange coppery metal. There's a long wooden staff in his hand The strange thing about him is he doesn't appear to be completely solid. Now and then, when the light hits him just right, you can see through him. It reminds you of when Kayla faded out before the battle with the blood grubs.

He seems to notice the strange look on your faces and laughs. "You've realized I'm not quite all here, I gather."

Zack speaks first. "What's wrong with you? Is it a curse or something?"

Kayla and John exchange a somber look before he speaks. "We're all cursed in this place."

Kayla picks at a leaf. "We seem have only a certain amount of energy after we lose the game. The longer you're here, the less you have. John was here when I got here. There were others too, but they've faded out completely. Now there's only John, Finn, and I left.

"Finn?" you question. "Is he another player that got caught in the game?"

Kayla nods. "He's a loner, but he'll turn up sooner or later. He mostly keeps to the mountains."

This is a lot of new information to take in. The fact that there have been others trapped in this world makes you question your chances of success. Turning to Kayla, you try to clarify. "When you were talking before, you said they 'faded.' What does that mean?"

John speaks first. "This place doesn't exist in the regular world. It's a space between time, so when you die in the game, there's no real place for you to go.

We're not completely sure, but what we think is you have to stay here until your mortal life would have been finished, and then you fade out for good."

Zack adjusts his glasses. "Then where do you go?"

"Another question we can't answer, but wherever it is, you finally leave the game." John rubs a hand over Goliath's massive head. "My flickering appearance means I'll disappear completely soon."

You can see the sadness on Kayla's face when he mentions fading out. You realize how lonely you would be in this world without Zack. Ismael swoops down at that moment and lands delicately on her shoulder, coaxing a smile from her.

"There used to be more people coming in all the time," John said. "But since Kayla came, we haven't seen anyone new until you."

Zack thinks for a minute. "That's probably because of Old Man Larsen's fence. He gated the whole area off."

"Did you say Larsen?" Kayla asked breathlessly. "That's my last name."

Zack squints and pushes up his glasses. "Then

Mr. Larsen must be—"

"He's my dad!" Kayla yells. "He found a way to stop it. He promised he would."

"Your dad?" you say, trying to put all the pieces together. "How is that possible? He's an old man."

"We don't age in the game," John explains. "Whatever age we are when we . . . well, when we lose. That's the age we stay."

You look to Kayla. "Your dad was in the game, too?"

She nods. "We got caught in here together. That horrible cat creature came, and we got separated. He must have made it through because I never saw him in here, but I never knew for sure. Is he okay?"

You think a minute before answering. "Well, he's mean and has a limp, but I guess he's okay. I always thought he was crazy, but now I suppose he's a hero, keeping The Gamekeeper from trapping anyone else in here."

Kayla is practically beaming. She takes your hands, earning you a scowl from Zack. "You have to finish the game and get out. You need to let him know I'm still here, but I'm okay. He must be so worried, never knowing what happened to me. I'm fifteen forever, but I'm okay. I have Ismael here and John and even Finn, although he's sort of a pain."

She paces back and forth on the grass as she talks. Her face is reflective, almost as if she's talking more to herself than to you. "I've had other friends here, too.

There was Margaret, before she faded, and some others. They were good to me." She turns, focusing on your face. "You have to tell him I'm happy. I wish I would have gotten out, but let him know I'm okay."

"We have to find a way to get you out," Zack says.

Kayla shakes her head. "That's not possible. Just tell him I'm okay." She throws her arms around your neck. "I'm just so happy."

Zack's scowls at you and then holds out his arms.

She turns to hug him next, but then her face changes and she seem to come to a realization and drops her arms. "You two need to get moving. If you don't reach the cave before nightfall, you'll never make to the end. Believe me, you don't want to be out here when it's dark. That's when the really bad things come out."

Zack's face falls as she pushes you both back toward the path.

"Get to the cave," she says. "You'll be safe there."

CHAPTER 8

You pass the canteen to Zack as you hike along the trail toward the next cave.

His face has been a dark cloud for the last half hour. "I can't believe she hugged you."

"It didn't mean anything. She was just excited about her dad."

"I suppose you're right—but it doesn't mean I have to like it." He doesn't say any more, but after a few more minutes, the scowl starts to fade from his face. "I feel kind of bad about Kayla's dad. Everybody thinks he's some crazy old geezer, but his fence kept people safe from The Gamekeeper for a long time."

You snort and punch Zack in the arm. "Yeah, until a couple of geniuses saw the lock was off and decided they had to find out what was inside."

Zack laughs, but then his face drops. "You still think we're going to make it out. Don't you?"

You have no idea, but you can tell Zack's counting on you. "Definitely. Besides, our stones are almost full, so we'll have the wolf with us soon."

"I'll be glad to have him in our corner again. I didn't think we were going to make it through that last battle."

You examine a cut on your arm from one of the pinchers. "I know. That was intense. You felt it though, right? The weapons— they have some kind of power in them."

"Of course I felt it," Zack says. "And good thing. Otherwise, we'd be a pile of worm poop by now."

"I don't understand. This world is weird. It's supposed to be designed to kill us, but then The Gamekeeper gives us these weapons and armor that totally save us.

You recognize the voice of The Gamekeeper before you see him. "Are you complaining there's too much to keep you alive? It's a bit ungrateful. Don't you think?"

Looking around, you spot him leaning against a tree not far down the path. "Did you give us the armor?"

He points a spindly finger at you. "The trouble with you humans is you think yourselves too important. This game has existed for centuries."

He waves his hands, and purple smoke swirls around them. It forms into a foggy version of an old-fashioned scale and hovers in the air.

"It is a game, after all," he says, "and like any good game, it has to be balanced. It's not fun to win if it isn't on a fair playing field." The Gamekeeper conjures little wooden figures of crows and worms. He places them on the scale. Then he places a wooden replica of the wolf on the opposite side. "So, there must be things here that kill you and things here that help you."

"Like the Guardians?" Zack says.

He looks at Zack with a sneer and waves away the smoky scale. "Yes, like the Guardians. Apparently, you've been talking to one of my pets." He starts moving toward you.

"Pets?" Zack asks quietly.

You lean closer and whisper, "I think he means people stuck in the game, like Kayla." You remember that he said Ashley might end up as a pet and a new flood of worry washes over you.

The Gamekeeper steps closer "I wonder which one it was. They're supposed to be impartial.

However, most are still a bit put out they can't go home, so heed the information you receive from them with caution. I don't want them steering you into quicksand and ruining my fun."

Directly in front of you now, he places a hand on each of your foreheads. A blinding pain flashes through your skull, and you hear Zack cry out. Your legs feel like all the energy is being pulled from them until you fall to your knees.

An image of Ashley sitting on a throne made of what looks like bones flashes into your mind. There are plates of food and chests of jewels and gold surrounding her. Little goblin creatures are giving her things and combing through her hair.

The Gamekeeper's voice presses into your mind. "You can see that she's cared for, fed, clothed. I've made her a queen. All you have to do is go back. Leave her and return to your life."

You struggle to speak. "Not . . . without. . . Ashley."

He releases his touch, and you and Zack collapse to the ground, panting.

The Gamekeeper clucks his tongue. "I was afraid

of this. You got the wolf, then the weapons. I knew you'd think it was possible to get through. So, I came to demonstrate what you *don't* know."

Slowly your strength returns, and you help Zack to his feet.

"You keep getting all this false hope," The Gamekeeper says. He waves his arm, and smoke forms a wavering circle in the air. "You need to know what is still out there."

Huge fanged animals and creatures you hadn't even imagined in your nightmares flash across the circle as if on a projection screen. You don't want to appear weak, but the images are terrible, and you can't help shrinking back.

"You need to give up," The Gamekeeper says, his voice dripping with sympathy. "Let me send you home. You can't do this."

Your hands are shaking. You can't beat those things. Kayla said she's happy here. Maybe Ashley could learn to be happy here, too. You stare at the ground, unsure what to do next.

The Gamekeeper smiles. "I see you're coming to your senses. Now let me just tell you how to get out."

"No!" Zack's defiant voice surprises you and seems to have a similar effect on The Gamekeeper.

"What did you say?" The Gamekeeper questions.

Zack pulls his axe out of the scabbard and readies himself for battle. "I said, 'No.' And Kayla isn't your pet."

You look up at him. "Zack, I—"

His face is stone. "Don't you dare let him win now. I'm terrified, but if you say we can do it, I can believe we'll win."

Your shoulders slump. "I'm not sure we can anymore. What about those things he showed us? Those monsters?"

Zack gestures to the forest. "So, there are crazy things out there. They've always been there. It's the same game we already started. At least we know what's coming. Now get up, get out your sword, and let's get through this stupid game."

Zack has a point. You square your shoulders and draw your sword.

The Gamekeeper sneers. "A very emotional little pep talk, but my creatures will still be too strong for you."

Suddenly, something The Gamekeeper said before clicks in your head. "It's a game," you say to Zack.

He gives you a questioning look.

"He said the game has to be fair. So that means there is just as much power out there to save us as there is to kill us."

A smile creeps across Zack's lips.

New determination pushes away your fear. "You're right. We *can* do this. Now let's get going." You and Zack walk past The Gamekeeper and continue down the overgrown path.

He chuckles from behind you. "Inspiring to be sure, but no matter what you think you understand about this world, it still belongs to me."

You keep walking without so much as a flinch in his direction.

The Gamekeeper's voice is crazed with anger now. "You think you've got it all figured out. But I hold all the cards. I will make sure you never win, and unlike my other playthings I let romp around the woods with their little animals, I have something very special in mind for you two."

You keep your eyes focused on the path in front of you. The Gamekeeper's voice grows more distant with each step.

"Since my world no longer scares you, I'll call up something very special. You made your choice. There's no going back. You are mine." He pauses and then yells the last word as a wave of energy explodes from him. "FOREVER!"

The blast almost knocks you to the ground, but it's the ensuing silence that's truly terrifying. The forest has gone still. Not a bird twitters. Not a sound can be heard.

From the darkness of the trees behind you, you hear a low growl. Glowing eyes appear, first one pair— then another— and another.

You and Zack back toward the cliff face. One of the creatures emerges from the shadows of the trees. Although the shape is dog-like, the creature is more nightmare than man's best friend. Its flat boxy head makes it resemble a hyena with no fur. Instead, it's covered with what looks like rotten, oozing flesh.

Its eyes are milky, and drool drips from snarling jaws. A rim of bony spikes, also covered with tightly-stretched, decaying meat, forms a spiny collar behind its neck. Several pairs of eyes are in front of you, and you can see more of the beasts coming out of the trees.

With your back against the cliff face, you pull out your sword. Zack readies his axe. The putrid stench of the animals makes your eyes water. Bile rises in your throat, and you fight a wave of nausea.

The lead creature presses slowly toward you, its pack close behind. You glance at your valor stone, wishing it was full enough to summon the wolf. The leader snarls and snaps as it inches toward you. You swing your sword, but the creature jumps back, giving a strangled bark.

The rest of the pack paces behind its alpha leader. Once the first one attacks, the entire pack will probably follow. With just Zack at your side, you're not sure you'll be able to fend them all off, no matter what kind of weapons you have.

Above you, on the cliff, you hear something moving. Dirt and rock sift down.

Zack's eyes dart up. "Are there more up there?"

You shrug, unsure you even want to know.

Something drops from the cliff. Zack swings his axe, but a shield blocks his blow. Instead of a dog, you see a boy, not much older than you, with a sword and shield.

"Get back," he yells, pushing his shield in front of himself. He blocks you from the attack with his shield and slices at the dogs with a glowing blue dagger, forcing them back a bit.

He talks to you over his shoulder. "We have one shot at this. When I give the signal, you two run. No questions, no looking back. You have a quarter mile to the cave. If you can beat them to it, you'll be safe."

"Who are you?" you ask.

He shakes his head. "No time. Get ready."

A thundering boom echoes from the side of the cliff above you. Blinding blue light knocks the dogs back, completely blasting the closest two animals into piles of decomposing meat.

"Now!" the boy yells. He begins to fade out. When you see him flicker, you realize he must be someone who lost the game.

You and Zack run, tearing through the trees and underbrush to escape.

Soon you hear grunts and yaps behind you again. They must have recovered from whatever that blast was. You have a good lead, but they're faster and catching up rapidly. Vines snag against your weapons, and thorns and branches rip at your clothes.

"There!" Zack points to a dark spot on the cliff not far from you. The cave entrance is just a few yards away.

The stench of the dog's rotting flesh surrounds you. They must be nearly on you again. You hear them snapping and growling, but you can't look back. The cave is so close. With everything you have left, you push for the cavern and dive through the opening. Zack follows, landing on top of you as you clear the doorway. One of the creatures jumps through the opening. As its body enters the cave's mouth, it bursts into flames, leaving only a pile of ash. Another two dogs meet a similar fate.

Outside, the pack snaps and snarls. One even sniffs the edge of the doorway but yelps when its nose is singed by an invisible forcefield. Above the door, you notice symbols carved into the stone.

"They're runes," you say. "I saw them once in a

book. They must keep the dark stuff out."

Another dog snaps its jaws across the threshold only to meet a burning reward.

Zack stares at the opening. "I love runes. I don't know what they are, but if they keep those things out, then runes are my new favorite thing."

You point to the markings that surround the cave mouth. "They must have mystical power or something. I saw them once in a movie, but I never thought they were real."

"Most of the things we've seen today aren't supposed to be real, so I guess it makes sense," Zack says. "Let's look around."

Another large jewel, just like the one in the first cave, glows from its place near the back of the cavern. Though similar, this cave is much bigger. A small waterfall gushes from a crevice in the rocks.

You follow it with your eye and see it feeds a river that runs through the length of the cave. After a cautious taste, Zack pronounces the water okay to drink, and you fill your canteen.

There's a shelf-like ledge under the glowing jewel and beneath, another cache. This time, instead of swords and axes, you find leather arm and leg bracers, shields, and a small leather bag.

"Yes," Zack says, pulling out new leg armor. "No more towel boy." He looks inside the small bag and finds some crackers and dates. As you make a small pile of armor, you catch a glint from something near the bottom of the cache. It's a pendant in the shape of a large brass eye.

"Whoa," Zack says. "What is that?"

"I don't know." You hold it up to the light. "It looks just like the wolf's eye."

"You mean our wolf?" Zack examines it more closely. "You're right. Definitely our wolf."

"So, you think we're supposed to take it?"

"You can if you want to," Zack says, taking a small bite of one the crackers. "I never wear anything around my neck since I almost hung myself with a superman cape when I was seven. Besides, it feels like it should belong to *you*."

"Why do you say that?"

"I don't know," he answers. "Just a feeling."

You don't say anything, but you can't deny you feel drawn to this piece. You slip it over your neck.

As you do, a surge of power seems to zip up your spine.

Zack doesn't seem to notice the exchange of power. He's looking at the armor and food.

"These cracker things are pretty good," he says and holds out a piece for you.

Unable to explain what you experienced, you take the food and eat it slowly. "We probably better conserve food. We don't know when we'll have food again."

"You pick up a pair of bracers and replace your towel version with them. It feels awkward but slightly electrifying. The weapons must increase in power as they're combined. You look at Zack. "Team wolf is starting to look like something to worry about."

THE CRACKERS IN THE CAVE ARE ENCHANTED. ROLL THE DICE. IF YOU GET 1, 2, OR 4, YOU GAIN 5 EXTRA LIFE POINTS.

CHAPTER 9

You wake from a night of horrible dreams featuring a jumble of the scales, fangs, matted fur, and bloody talons The Gamekeeper showed you through his smoky circle. Dust-filled beams of morning sun pour through the cave entrance.

The runes are still glowing. You sigh, remembering where you are. You're thankful to be safe for now, but this whole game is a nightmare you can't wake up from. You try to stretch and realize that Zack is curled up on your shoulder.

Drool stretches from the corner of his mouth to your tee-shirt.

"Ugh." You push him off.

Zack sits up and reaches for his axe, instantly on guard. "What's wrong? Did those things get in?"

You point at the puddle on your shirt. "You drooled on me. And we don't cuddle—*ever*! Got it?"

Zack smiles and wipes at the corner of his mouth. "It's not like I planned it."

Laughter comes from the back of the cave.

You scramble to your feet with Zack right behind

you, each grabbing for your weapon.

The boy from the battle yesterday jumps down from the small ledge above the cache.

You take a defensive stance as Zack readies his axe.

The stranger walks slowly toward you. "Relax, ladies. If I'd wanted to hurt you, I would have done it during nap time." As he comes out of the shadows, you can see his dimpled, dirty face and messy brown hair sprouting from the top of his head like a strange plant.

"Who are you?" Your voice sounds steady, but your heart is still pounding.

"The name's Finn," he says, giving a short bow. "At your service." He's heavily armored, and the clash between his warrior look and boyish face are almost funny.

You recognize the name. "Finn? We've heard about you. Kayla and John told us you were around."

"My reputation precedes me then?

You nod "Are you the one who helped us yesterday?"

"In a way, but Sampson played a more vital role

in it than I did. He gestures to a large mound of white fur next to him which he nudges with his foot. It uncurls to reveal a large ram with huge coiled horns.

The ram pushes against Finn's legs affectionately then clambers to its feet. You notice his horns crackle with blue lightning. Finn rubs the animal's shaggy head, and the ram affectionately butts him.

"That's your protector?" Zack asks. He reaches out to touch the rams head with a hesitant hand and receives a jolt.

Finn smiles with obvious pride. "He's a moody brute but good to have around in a battle. Kinda like me in that regard."

You hear yips and growls from outside the cave

Sampson snorts and paws at the ground until Finn pats his back. "Easy, boy. You'll have your chance."

Zack turns toward the entrance. "Those dog things are still there?"

Finn keeps a calming hand on Sampson's neck. "You must have made a real enemy of The Gamekeeper for him to send his personal guard against you. Flesh hounds are nasty things."

"Everything here is nasty," you say.

"True enough, but these guys don't just rip you up. Flesh hounds are especially troublesome because they steal bits of your soul."

Zack swallows hard. "Did you say they steal your soul?"

Finn laughs.

You lean toward Zack. "He's just trying to mess with us."

"Like half-decayed attack dogs aren't enough?" Zack says. He turns to Finn. "How long before they leave?"

"Leave?" Finn snorts. "Maybe you didn't hear me. These beasts are The Gamekeeper's personal guard. They know his cruelty better than anyone. They aren't going back to him without bits of you in their jaws."

So, are we supposed to hide in this cave forever?" you say.

"Pssshhh," Finn hisses. "You're thinking about this all wrong. In this world, you're warriors, and warriors don't hide behind the safety of the runes forever. You've had a rest and are armored up. What more are you waiting for? Take a deep breath and grab your weapons. It's time to battle."

You turn your sword and study your valor stone. It's full and glowing. You show Zack. "The valor stones seem to think the same thing. Let's call the wolf."

At the mention of his name, the huge animal appears. He rubs against you and then Zack. He sniffs toward Finn and Sampson and gives a throaty growl.

You run a hand along his back. "Easy, boy, we're on the same team." You nod toward the cave entrance. "The enemy is out there."

As if on cue, or perhaps stirred by the scent of the wolf, the flesh hounds start to bay loudly.

Finn pulls a dagger from a holster on his thigh and picks up his shield. "All right, boys, I won't last long as I've grown rather transparent lately, but Sampson and I will give you all we've got."

You turn toward the mouth of the cave and glance at Zack. "Are we ready for this?"

"Do we have a choice?" he asks.

You tighten the leather bracers on your arms. "Fraid not."

"Then I guess we're as ready as we're ever going to be," he says, readying his axe.

You feel the hot breath of the wolf behind you. "Let's hope it's enough."

CHAPTER 10

Blue lightning shoots out from Sampson's horns as he butts at the air. The wave of energy sizzles the flesh of the closest dog and knocks the others back. You burst from the cave behind the blast zone with Zack, Finn, and the wolf beside you.

Finn's dagger and shield are a blur against the snapping jaws. He swings his shield, and it connects with the nearest creature's muzzle. You hear the crack of bone as it snaps. Spinning again, he jabs his blade at the middle of another flesh hound, puncturing the putrid flesh.

The wolf corners one of the hounds against the mountain while you and Zack swing your weapons against other members of the pack.

Your sword slices through one of the creatures, and you watch it slump to the ground. Your group is doing some major damage, but the flesh hounds aren't giving up. The pack continues to close in surrounding you.

Finn takes out another with a slice of his dagger and blocks an attack with his shield. He laughs as

Sampson's massive head knocks four of the dogs through the air and slams them into the side of the mountain. You see both Sampson and Finn flicker. The ram butts a snarling animal toward you, and you use your sword to finish it.

"I'm afraid that's about all for us boys," Finn says. "Good luck." They gradually fade away, taking out dogs until they disappear completely.

The fear of fighting without them distracts you, and your sword dips. One of the creatures clamps its jaws around your arm. Thankfully, the leather bracer protects you from the bite, but the dog is strong, and his violent shaking threatens to break your arm.

You involuntarily cry out. Your left hand isn't strong enough to swing the sword. You try to push the flesh hound off, but your hand peels through its cankered skin. Putrefied meat and puss cover your fingers like a sticky glove. The smell gags you. Your armor buzzes, and you know its power is protecting you even in this dangerous situation.

With a yelp, the wolf rips the rotting dog away and flings its lifeless body into the bushes. You recover your sword and slash at the remaining dogs.

There are so many of them. Zack and the wolf are fighting hard against the pack, but even all together, you’re not sure you can beat creatures like these.

YOU KNOW THE DRILL.

ROLL THE DIE TO SEE THE BATTLE UNFOLD. IF YOU HAVE THE ELEMENTAL SWORD OR THE FIRE SWORD ADD A WOUND TO EACH ROLL OF 2 OR 3.

IF YOU HAVE THE LIGHTNING SWORD, SAMPSON'S POWERS BOOST ITS ENERGY. THE HOUNDS TAKE DOUBLE WOUNDS WITH A ROLL OF 1,4, OR 6.

Roll	1	2	3	4	5	6
Flesh Hound Wounds	1	2	4	5	6	6
Your Wounds	5	5	4	3	3	2

THE FLESH HOUNDS START WITH 15 LIFE POINTS. SUBTRACT WOUNDS ACCORDING TO THE CHART.

15 - ____=_______.

TRANSFER LIFE POINTS FROM THE LAST BATTLE PAGE, AND THEN SUBTRACT WOUNDS.

(TRANSFERRED POINTS- WOUNDS = NEW LIFE POINTS)

_______ -_____= ______.

IF THE HOUNDS' POINTS REACH 0, YOU HAVE WON THIS BATTLE. KEEP ROLLING AND SUBTRACTING UNTIL THE HOUNDS ARE DEFEATED.

GO TO THE LAST PAGE IF YOU RUN OUT OF POINTS. WHEN YOU DEFEAT THE FLESH HOUNDS, WRITE THE NUMBER OF POINTS YOU HAVE LEFT HERE ________. YOU CAN USE THEM FOR FUTURE BATTLES.

CHAPTER 11

Somehow you made it through the battle with the hounds. You squat next to the river inside the cave, trying to wash yourself off. The stench of decay clings to you from the flesh hounds. The battle was fierce, but at least the wolf got to stay.

Zack scrubs at his arms next to you. He hesitantly gives them a sniff. "Whoo wee. Those dogs put off some serious stink. I would give a lot for a bar of soap right now."

"I think even skunk would be an improvement," you say. You use the sand from the bottom of the river to scour your hands, and it seems to help a little. After scrubbing until your skin is raw, you gather your armor and put it back on. It's hard to tell if you actually smell better or if you're getting used to it. As you lift your sword to put it in the scabbard, you take note of your valor stone. It's empty.

Zack hands you one of the crackers from the leather pouch you found. They're not exactly the saltines you're used to, but they're not bad, and they're surprisingly filling for something so small. "I wonder if there are more caves we're supposed to find?"

"Seems logical that there would be," Zack says, reclining back against the cave wall.

"I wish there were some kind of map we could use. It would be a lot easier to get to The Gamekeeper's castle if we knew where it was."

Zack laces his fingers behind his head. "Kayla and the others are around. So far, they've steered us the right way. I guess we'll have to let them be our map for now."

You rise from the ledge and start to fill the backpack. "That's true, but something that The Gamekeeper said has been bothering me about them."

Zack looks confused.

"Remember, he said that some of the people in the game are angry about being here? He also said they might try to get us killed. So now I'm not sure we can trust anyone but each other."

Zack narrows his eyes. "We can trust Kayla. The Gamekeeper is just trying to freak us out."

"Maybe ,but we don't really know these people."

A slow grin spreads across Zack's lips. "Good point. We should spend some more time with Kayla and really get to know her."

You shake your head. "I think we need to be more careful about listening to them. We need to take care of ourselves. They're already stuck in the game. We don't want to end up here, too, no matter how cute she is."

You and Zack quickly finish packing and start down the tree-lined walkway away from the cave. You follow the path as the sun's position marks the passing hours. Zack's been moody since your conversation about Kayla. You change the subject to get his mind off her. "I've been thinking. We need to give the wolf a name."

Zack considers the idea. "Yeah, I guess now that he's part of our team, we should probably have something to call him."

"How about Fluffy?" you offer, hoping it will make Zack laugh, which it does.

"You can call him Fluffy if you want, but he'll probably eat you."

"Good point. How about Tarzan?"

"Nah, that's apes not dogs."

"Nanook? Kujo?"

Zack pulls a face. "You're terrible at this. I think you should stop before you hurt yourself."

"I blame my parents. They never let me have a pet."

"It needs to be something tough," Zack says, "but intelligent."

You study the etching around the edge of the pendant. You flip it over and see that there is another rune carved into the metal. "How about Spirit?"

"That's better, but it doesn't seem quite right. I wonder if he already has a name?"

As your thumb runs over the rune on the back, the pendant seems to pulse in your hand. A name drifts into your mind like a whisper. "Gunnolf," you say, not knowing how it got into your head. "Gunnolf is his name."

Zack stares at you. "Okay. I guess that works."

"It's his name."

"How do you know?"

"I can't explain it, but somehow, I know." An image of him hunting alongside fearsome, Viking warriors flashes into your head. You drop the pendant, and the image disappears like mist wiped from a mirror.

The landscape has gradually changed over the course of the day. Though the trees remain on the left side of you, the area on the right has become a muddy swamp with short, spiked vegetation and bubbling pools of mud. A foul sulfur smell wafts up from the swampy water.

Zack's face contorts. "Ugh, do you smell that?"

"I thought it was you."

He looks insulted. "If I smelled like that, I'd be rotting from the inside out."

Wet, gassy sounds come from bubbling mud next to the path.

You wave a hand in front of your nose. "Oh man, that's disgusting."

"Yeah," Zack says. "There must be some underground hot springs close by to cause the smell. It's sulfur releasing from the mud."

You groan. "If this is part of the plan to kill us, I think it's working."

Zack laughs. "I can hear it now. They survived

the blood grubs and the flesh hounds, but it was the farting mud that got them."

From the corner of your eye, you see a large ripple in the watery sludge. You stop. "Did you see that?" As you stare out at the bog, the bubbles seem to be getting larger.

"I don't think I'm going to like where this goes," Zack says. "Should we make a run for it?"

A strange warmth spreads from the wolf eye pendant, and you feel strongly that you should take a stand here. "We need to stay put."

Soon shapes rise out of the mud. You can make out the hunched shoulders of a dark figure, then another, rising from the swampy muck. "Zack?"

"Yeah, I see it," he says. "I don't like it, but I see it."

You squint, trying to make sense of the shapes rising out of the bog. "What are those?"

"I'm not sure, but I'll bet they're gonna try to kill us."

"What else?" you say, reaching for your sword. You think of Gunnolf but realize you don't have enough valor tokens. The figures continue to rise from the slimy water until you can see that the shapes are human-like in form.

An army of dripping creatures stands before you. The mud and vegetation slide from their bony shoulders. Empty sockets glow red in the face of a skeleton warrior dressed in full armor. He raises his sword, and the rest turn to face you.

Zack whimpers next to you. "This is totally going to ruin Halloween for me—forever."

You nod. "Things are about to get interesting."

CHAPTER 12

Dozens of crimson eyes shine through the shadows. The skeletons' jaws gape, releasing low moans and grunts. Each corpse warrior is outfitted with a short sword in a scabbard and a decaying wooden shield with a symbol of a boar on it.

Zack tightens his grip on his axe. "I know we don't have enough valor tokens for the wolf, but I sure wish Finn or Kayla were here to fight, too."

"I agree. Look at those swords. We've never fought anything that has a weapon."

He gives a nervous laugh. "Remember the good old days when the biggest thing we'd ever killed was a daddy long leg spider?"

One of the group lowers his sword, and the army lumbers through the bog toward you. The sludge and moss of the swampy land slows their progress.

"So, we just wait while those things close in on us?" Zack says.

You search for an escape route. "We could run back the way we came, but I don't think we'd get too far before they caught up. Besides, then we'd risk having to fight them along a narrower part of the path." You wipe a sweaty hand on your pants then regrip your sword hilt. "I hate this waiting. There has to be a way to take some of them out while they're still wading across that bog."

"Another reason I wish Kayla were here," Zack says. Almost before he finishes the sentence, Kayla and John materialize next to you, weapons ready.

She winks at Zack. "Did someone invite us to the party?"

"Normally, we don't get involved in the business of the game," John explains. "Kayla insisted." He looks annoyed, but Kayla doesn't seem to care.

"Will Finn be coming, too?" you ask.

She narrows her eyes and juts out her chin. "Finn only does what he wants — when he wants. He can be quite a pill sometimes." She nocks an arrow in her bow then wrinkles her nose. "Ugh, that smell is killing me."

"For the record," Zack says, "that smell is not us."

You glance again at the advancing army of undead soldiers and shake your head. "Way to worry about the important things, buddy."

"The smell is part of a curse," Kayla says. She fires off a couple of arrows as she explains. "An ancient army rose up against The Gamekeeper. When they were defeated, he brought them here. Now he forces them to battle for him in this stink forever. You were smart to make a stand here. If you had gone any further down the path, they wouldn't have had the swamp to slow them down."

Kayla's arrows fly true, hitting several of the skeletons. They stagger backward but don't stop. She furrows her brow. "I'm barely doing any damage, and I'm going to fade soon. How do we beat these guys when they're already dead?"

Out of habit, you touch your wolf pendant. Within seconds an idea springs to your mind. "Maybe the question we should be asking is what's keeping them alive. How are they animated?"

Kayla's voice rises with excitement. "John, you told me about this legend. How does The Gamekeeper control them?"

He thinks for a moment. "He enchanted their leader's sword. I suppose if we kill him, the curse will break, and the entire army will drop."

You examine the army closely, trying to discern any differences in their gaunt forms. "They're exactly the same. How do we know which one is the leader now that they moved around?'

"We don't," John replies. "So, we have to take out as many as we can until they drop. I can lend Goliath to the fight, and I have a few tricks up my sleeve, yet, but I'm not going to last more than a few minutes in my condition."

Ismael flies down and lights on Kayla's shoulder. She has a short, whispered conversation with him, and then he starts to circle the army.

John lowers his voice and pulls you aside. He points beyond the skeletons. "When you get through this battle, you need to get to the next rune cave before dark. There's a fork in the road not far ahead. You need to stay to the right. Do you understand? *The right.*"

You nod. "I got it."

"It's very important," he says, grabbing your chest plate.

His intensity is a little alarming. You push his

hand away. "I don't exactly need GPS. Stay to the right's not that hard to understand."

Kayla looks over. "I don't know what's so important over there, but you guys need to get ready. Now!"

Ismael dives at the skeleton army, doing his corkscrew maneuver. Kayla is still firing, and between the two of them, they begin to do some serious damage to the skeletons' ranks. You haven't located the leader yet, though, so with every "kill" the soldiers keep reanimating.

Despite the valiant efforts of your little group, the skeletons have reached the rocky ground in front of you. The battle has arrived. Without the mud to hinder them, they advance quickly toward you.

Goliath appears. The large bear rushes past you into the battle. His massive paws take out multiple foes, leaving them in piles of discarded bones and armor.

John is right behind him, spinning his staff and striking targets with practiced grace. "Goliath, shockwave roar!" he shouts, and the bear lets out a deafening bellow. John grips his staff in both hands and slams it into the earth. A shockwave of blue light bursts from the staff. As the rings of light reach Goliath, it amplifies the bear's roar into a powerful sonic wave.

A large portion of the skeleton legion is blown to pieces, their bones scattered across the swamp. After only minutes, the skeletons begin to reform, each piece flying back to its original position like a film rewinding.

Goliath and John have faded out.

You block a sword with your shield and send a bony head flying with a swing of your own.

Ismael dives and spins, boring a path through the corpse warriors. Kayla has started to flicker, but she continues to send arrows into the fray. She hits one of the warriors near the shoulder and sends it to the ground. For a brief moment, all the warriors hesitate. They resume fighting as soon as the skeleton rises, the arrow still protruding from its collarbone. "There," Kayla yells, pointing at the marked soldier. "The one with the arrow." He's the leader."

The skeletons close ranks around their commander and begin to swarm around Kayla.

She's grown weak and nearly transparent. Zack moves to stand in front of her. He swings his axe like a scythe in a field, taking out five in quick succession with more fury than you've ever seen from him.

A warrior rises and lunges at you. You duck and then deliver a kick to his chest, knocking him back and off balance. A final swing from your sword sends his head to meet his brothers in the piles of bones that litter the ground around you.

Ismael speeds toward another group of warriors and begins his spin. He makes it through half of them but disappears before he can yield maximum affect.

Zack glances behind him as Kayla disappears. "We're on our own," he yells.

You nod. "I just hope you fight as hard for me as you did for that girl."

"Well, I can't promise anything," he says. "You're really not as cute. But, since I'm not a big fan of death by skeleton, let's beat these boneheads."

BATTLE TIME.

IF YOU HAVE A FROST SWORD OR AN ELEMENTAL SWORD, THE SKELETONS TAKE DOUBLE WOUNDS ON A ROLL OF 2 OR 4.

THE LIGHTNING SWORD HURTS YOU IN THIS BATTLE BECAUSE IT STRENGTHENS THE SKELETONS. IF YOU HAVE IT, SUBTRACT 2 ADDITIONAL WOUNDS FROM YOUR LIFE POINTS EACH TIME A 6 IS ROLLED.

Roll	1	2	3	4	5	6
Skeleton Warriors	2	2	3	5	6	6
Your Wounds	6	4	3	2	1	1

THE SKELETON WARRIORS START WITH TWELVE LIFE POINTS. SUBTRACT THE WOUNDS THEY GET ACCORDING TO THE CHART AND WRITE IT HERE

12 - ____=_______.

TRANSFER YOUR LIFE POINTS FROM THE LAST BATTLE PAGE. SUBTRACT YOUR WOUNDS ACCORDING TO THE ROLL AND WRITE IT HERE.

________ -______= ______.

IF THE SKELETONS' POINTS REACH 0, YOU HAVE WON THIS BATTLE. WRITE THE NUMBER OF POINTS YOU HAVE LEFT HERE ________ TO USE FOR FUTURE BATTLES.

KEEP ROLLING AND SUBTRACTING UNTIL THE SKELETONS ARE DEFEATED. SUBTRACT YOUR OWN WOUNDS FOR EACH ROLL.

GO TO THE LAST PAGE IF YOU RUN OUT OF POINTS.

CHAPTER 13

John was right. Once you take out the leader, vanquishing the rest of them is easy. Zack smashes the final skeleton into bits with his axe. Its head rolls across the path and into the putrid bog. As it slowly sinks back into the muck, the red glow fades from the empty sockets.

The bubbling mud makes a particularly loud farting sound, and you and Zack can't help but laugh. "I guess the bog wanted to have the last word," you say.

Zack wrinkles up his nose. "Isn't the smell enough. I wish I had some beans so that I could fight back."

Piles of skeleton bones are all around you. You nudge one with your shoe. "I think we've done enough fighting back for now. Besides, I've smelled you after you have beans, and it wouldn't be a fair contest."

Pieces of tarnished, rusting armor and yellowed bones litter the path. Zack picks up a fallen sword and examines it. "Now that these things aren't trying to kill us, I feel kind of bad. Once upon a time, they tried to fight against The Gamekeeper. They used to be the good guys."

You push a shield away from the pale hand of a fallen warrior with your sword. "If The Gamekeeper made me one of his puppets, I'd rather be killed. At least it would be a release." Warmth spreads across your chest from the pendant, putting you on alert. Seconds later, the dark laughter of The Gamekeeper echoes through the trees.

He appears at the edge of the swamp, blocking your path. "I'll keep that in mind when you lose. Don't worry, though. That army challenged me centuries ago. I've matured ever so much since then." He wears an arrogant smirk. "How are you, boys? It seems like ages since we've talked."

You try to walk around him. "I thought something stunk around here. We didn't miss you, if you're wondering."

The Gamekeeper feigns shock. "And I thought we were becoming friends." He moves subtly left to block your path. "Don't rush off. We have loads to catch up on. You know, only a few of my hounds came back yesterday. Is that any way to treat the locals?"

"Do you want us to apologize?" Zack asks.

The Gamekeeper's expression remains unsettlingly calm as his eyes narrow into an icy glare. "Oh, not now." He laughs. "Believe me there will be plenty of time to regret *all* your decisions. Today, I came to warn you. I noticed some of the other players have been helping you."

You adjust your scabbard. "There isn't any rule about that."

He pushes a piece of his long, dark hair behind his ear with a spindly finger. "No. Of course there isn't, but you should know that one of them means to betray you. I told you not to trust them."

This is something that has been bothering you since The Gamekeeper mentioned it before. What if it's true and you and Zack are walking right into a trap? No. You can't let The Gamekeeper get to you. All he does is lie. You turn to your friend. "Don't listen to him, Zack. How would he even know that?"

Several of the crows fly over the trees. They perch in the branches next to The Gamekeeper.

"Let's just say. . ." He holds out an arm, and a crow climbs onto his shoulder. ". . . a little bird told me."

Zack's face contorts with rage. "I don't believe you."

The Gamekeeper rubs his hands together. "I knew you wouldn't. That's what makes it so much fun. You humans have this adorable habit of believing people are naturally good and then trusting them completely. It's like shooting fish in a barrel."

Even though The Gamekeeper terrifies you, you can't stand him trying to manipulate you. "We don't need your help."

His eyes reflect pure hatred. "Oh, if only that were true." He laughs, then lower's his voice to a threatening whisper. "When this is over, and you *finally* realize that you can't beat me, I promise you'll beg for my help." He raises his arms, and the crows all fly up into the air, forming a funnel cloud of black. The Gamekeeper disappears into the swirl of feathers.

Zack secures his axe into the leather strap across his back and kicks some of the bones out of his path. "Can't he walk off like a normal person? Always so much drama."

You shoot your friend a thankful look for breaking the tension. "At least he didn't sick some terrible beast on us this time."

"Yeah, he didn't even throw dirt at us. Why do you suppose that is?"

You nudge his shoulder. "I don't know. Maybe he finally got an eyeful of your beefy man muscles and decided he was no match for us." You put your sword away and walk in the direction of the cave. As you approach a narrow part of the path that skirts the edge of the bog, you ask, "Do you really think Kayla and the others might be plotting to betray us?"

Zack looks horrified. "Kayla would never do that."

"Oh, because you've known her for so long?" You turn sideways and slide-step around a particularly narrow part of the path where the mountain juts out.

Zack follows suit. "No, because she's saved our butts like three times."

You decide to change the subject. He simply can't be reasonable when it comes to Kayla. Pointing at the narrow pathway you say, "I'm glad we didn't try to run. It would have been hard to fight them here.

"Yeah, good call."

You think about the pulse from the pendant and wonder if was only in your mind. You're tempted to tell Zack about it, but you have no proof. You continue to slide around the foul bog. "Think you'd ever get used to this smell?"

Zack screws up his face. "Doubt it."

Only when you both reach the safety of the widening path do you say, "It's a good thing you didn't fall in. Then not only would you be trapped here, but you'd smell like a giant fart for all eternity. Kayla would only come near you if she wore a clothespin on her nose."

A look of horror crosses his face. "Dude. That's not funny."

You laugh because it's obvious he's more afraid of smelling like the farting bog and grossing out Kayla than actually getting trapped here. The path winds away from the sulfurous mud. It curves through a grove of willow trees that have large thorny barbs lining their thin branches. They slap at you every time the breeze blows, making their razor-sharp points difficult to avoid. One catches on your shirt, pulling you into several others. Zack untangles you, but a branch slaps at his face, leaving a bleeding gash.

After fighting through them for what feels like hours, you're covered in scratches and cuts. Eventually the trees thin and then disappear behind you.

Zack looks around. "Don't get me wrong. Those trees were enough for me, but doesn't it seems strange that there isn't anything with fangs chasing us?"

"It *has* been awhile since anything tried to kill us," you say. "Maybe this means we're in the middle. Like in a tornado, when it's calm in the eye of the storm."

He dabs at the blood on his cheek. "Maybe, but I was hoping we were closer to the end than that or at least closer to the cave. It'll be dark in a few hours."

You walk for another half mile or so before you notice a fork in the road up ahead.

"Which way should we go?" Zack asks.

"John told me to stay to the right." You both turn to head down the right side of the path.

Finn appears along the side of the road. "You must have the worst radar for survival of anyone I've ever met. You boys can't seem to keep out of trouble."

You shake your head. "What are you talking about?"

"You're heading down the wrong side. The cave is this way." He hooks a thumb to the left.

"But John specifically told me to stay to the right," you say.

Finn scratches his head. "Then he's either lying or stupid. I promise you don't want to go that way. It's like a sure ticket to sudden death."

Zack looks down the path. "Maybe you heard John wrong."

"John seemed pretty clear. He practically tattooed it on my forehead. He told me right before we fought the skeletons." You gesture to Zack. "You were there. Didn't you hear him?"

He shakes his head. "Sorry, I was watching Kayla fight." He looks down each path and then at Finn before turning to you. "What do you think we should do?"

"I'm telling you what to do!" Finn shouts. His ruddy face grows crimson. "Go to the left."

You look at Zack. Is this what The Gamekeeper was talking about? Is Finn trying to get you killed, or could it be John?

Zack must have been thinking along similar lines. "How do we know we can trust you?"

Finn juts out his chin. "Because I saved your skins." He sputters for a moment and then throws up his hands. "This is why I stay away from all of you freaks in the game. That's what got me stuck here in the first place, trying to save some stupid, ungrateful kid." He gives you a small salute. "Message received. You're on your own. When you die in this world, don't come looking for me to give you advice." He fades out, leaving you and Zack alone and more confused than ever.

"Wow," Zack says. "He was really mad."

"Yeah."

"So, do you still think we should stay to the right?"

You scan the two paths, but the same twisted trees and bushes line both.

"John says right, and Finn says left. I guess it comes down to which one we trust more."

"Well, you know how I feel about Kayla, and John's with her. Finn's such a hothead, and he admitted someone got him stuck in here. That would make anyone bitter."

Zack has a point, but now that you know The Gamekeeper wasn't lying, you have to be smart. "I do trust Kayla. I just wish she'd been the one to tell me instead of John. I don't know him well enough to determine his motives."

"It comes down to John or Finn," Zack repeats.

You take a deep breath. "I guess we go with John. He knows Kayla really wanted us to talk to her dad for her."

Zack puts up a hand. "Don't forget he also knows how much she likes me."

You give him a questioning look. "In that case, Romeo. I'm going to pray you have more animal magnetism than I think you do." You sigh. "We head right, but if we're wrong, you are never allowed to flirt again."

CHAPTER 14

Dense ferns and vegetation line the road John suggested. Zack seems completely confident in the decision, but you're still wary. Both of you start down the path with swords ready, a suggestion Zack doesn't exactly embrace.

After nearly twenty minutes without any sign of an attack, Zack places his axe in the scabbard against his back again. "I told you this was the right call."

"I guess so," you agree, but something about the path still bothers you. Hesitantly you follow his lead and put your sword away.

The sun penetrates through the dark trees in bursts of light, but mostly you're surrounded by shadows. Twisted vines dot the landscape now. They wrap around the trees and tangle along the rocks on the side of the road.

Zack shakes his head as he examines the vines. "These are weird. They don't even look like they belong in this forest."

A short laugh bursts from your lips. "We don't exactly belong here, either."

Further down the path, the vines get thicker. Purple flower-pods the size of basketballs, surrounded by menacing one-inch thorns, grow out of the vines at their thickest parts. A sweet, sickly smell comes from the flowers, and Zack seems too curious to ignore it. He stops to examine one of the larger pods.

"We don't have time for a science fair," you say. "We have to save Ashley."

"I know. I'm just looking. What harm is it going to do to look?"

"Haven't you ever seen a horror movie?" you say. "That's exactly what the characters always tell each other right before something terrible happens."

Zack rolls his eyes and continues to examine the plant. "This isn't a horror movie."

"No, it's worse," you say.

Zack raises his hands in surrender. "Good point." He starts to retreat. As he takes a step, you see him struggle. "Something has my leg." The vine has silently coiled around his calf. He reaches for his axe, but more vines slither around his arms and legs. The more Zack struggles, the faster the plant entraps him.

The snake-like vines grab you, too. You draw your sword but only manage to pull it in front of you before the vines pin your arms. The blade is trapped as the vines twist around your ankles and wrists like sinewy ropes. The thorns sting and burn, snagging at your clothes and skin at the gaps in your armor.

A now immobile Zack is being dragged toward the flower pods. He's right in front of one as it starts to open. "Help," he yells. Then a yellow cloud of something like pollen puffs from the plant. Instantly, he slumps to the ground.

You try to get to him, but the plant wraps around your legs tighter. It's pulling you closer and closer to one of the gaseous pods not far from where Zack collapsed. If you could only lift your arms, you could slice through the vine, but they're pinned in front of you by the twisting tendrils. At least your sword is still in your hand. You just need to get an arm free.

Ropes of green vine curl around your chest, making it difficult to breathe. In minutes, you'll be at the pod. It begins to open. Heat rises from the pendant against your chest, and an idea comes to your mind. The pod is the key. You use what little movement you have left in your arms to thrust your sword down into the middle of the flower. The whole plant seems to jump, and then the pod deflates. The vines release their hold.

You rip them from your arms and kick your feet wildly to get free. More vines reach out as you slash your way to Zack, but you hack them off before they can find a hold.

The twisting green tendrils have nearly swallowed Zack's prone form.

"Let him go," you say as your sword finds the middle of the pod that gassed him. The vines around you both shrink back. You slice at each thorny tentacle near you and puncture several surrounding pods.

YOU'RE ON YOUR OWN THIS TIME.

ROLL THE DIE AND SAVE YOUR FRIEND. LIKE ALWAYS, MATCH THE NUMBER ON THE DIE TO THE CHART. IF YOU HAVE A SHADOW BLADE, DOUBLE THE DAMAGE YOU DO TO THE PLANT.

IF YOU HAVE THE TIME SWORD AND ROLL 6 OR 2, TIME WILL REVERSE AND YOU GET BACK THE LAST TWO WOUNDS YOU TOOK.

Roll	1	2	3	4	5	6
Plant Wounds	2	3	3	4	5	6
Your Wounds	5	4	2	2	1	1

THE PLANT STARTS WITH TWELVE LIFE POINTS. SUBTRACT THE NUMBER OF WOUNDS ACCORDING TO THE CHART WRITE IT HERE 20 - ____=_______.

TRANSFER YOUR LIFE POINTS FROM THE LAST BATTLE PAGE. DON'T FORGET TO ADD ANY EXTRA LIFE POINTS YOU EARNED.

SUBTRACT THE NUMBER OF WOUNDS YOU TOOK ACCORDING TO THE ROLL AND WRITE IT HERE. (TRANSFERRED POINTS+ EXTRA LIFE POINTS - WOUNDS= NEW LIFE POINTS)_______ -_____= _____.

WHEN THE PLANT'S POINTS REACH 0, YOU HAVE WON THIS BATTLE. KEEP ROLLING AND SUBTRACTING UNTIL IT IS DEFEATED.

GO TO THE LAST PAGE IF YOU RUN OUT OF POINTS.WHEN YOU DEFEAT THE PLANT, WRITE THE NUMBER OF POINTS YOU HAVE LEFT HERE ________ TO USE FOR FUTURE BATTLES.

CHAPTER 15

After what seems like hours of slicing and stabbing, the plant swirls back into the deeper parts of the forest. Zack is lying on the ground. You slap his face lightly to try and get him to come around. A tense minute or two passes before he opens his eyes. He's groggy, but he's conscious. "What happened?" he says, touching his head.

"We found out, the hard way, you know nothing about plants or horror movies. I'm just glad to see you open your eyes. You really had me scared." Putting his arm around your shoulder, you help him stagger to a small clearing.

He leans his head back against the soft, cool moss. "Can we just stay here for a little while?"

He's so pale. You're still not sure what that pod did to him. He probably should sleep for a while, but you're afraid he might never wake up. "Come on Zack. I know you're tired, but we have to keep walking. Ashley needs us."

At the mention of Ashley, he struggles to his feet. Together you stumble down the path. Even with his arm around your shoulder again, he can barely walk. A light mist swirls around the trees, and the forest has gone eerily silent.

"I'm so cold," Zack says, through chattering teeth. The temperature has dropped a little, but it's more likely he's feeling an effect of the pod.

He's getting heavier and heavier, relying on you more as his own strength gives out. You're practically dragging him now. The mist gathers into a thick fog around your feet. It's difficult to see the path. Your arms and legs burn with exertion. At the next mossy patch, you let him slide to the ground, collapsing next to him as the mist envelops you.

His eyes are closed, and his breathing comes in shallow, panting breaths.

Taking him by the shoulders, you shake him. "Come on Zack, please wake up."

He stirs a little and mumbles something you can't make out, but his eyes stay closed.

Maybe some water will help flush the poison out of his system. You reach for the canteen but realize it isn't around his neck anymore. After looking around a bit, you see it lying on the path about ten feet away.

It's barely visible through the gathering mist until it glints in the sun. You edge toward the canteen, scouring the ground for any reappearance of the plant. You snatch it and head back to the spot where you left your friend only to find he's gone. There's no sign of him. He couldn't just disappear, could he?

"Zack!"

No answer.

You don't want to make too much noise. Who knows what else is waiting for you in the woods. Obviously, Finn was right. John led you into a trap.

You have to find Zack. Being in this horrible world is bad enough. Without your friend it's unbearable. You search near the path, climbing over and around huge fallen trees. The mist continues to swirl.

The sound of snapping tree limbs tells you something is close. Your valor stone is only about half full. You draw your sword and wait, ready to fight whatever comes at you. A single figure pushes through the trees.

It's Zack, and he's walking.

Relief washes over you. "Thank heavens. I've

been wandering around this place, and you have no idea what I had to. . .”

Zack is moving strangely, stumbling forward along the path.

You rush toward him. When you get about five feet away, you see his eyes are glazed, and drool is spilling from his mouth. “You better sit down, Zack. You don’t look too good.”

He stops walking and looks up, apparently drawn by your voice. He tilts his head in a strange, jerking movement as if he’s sizing you up. There is no recognition in his face. Suddenly, he reaches back and pulls his axe from the scabbard. It whizzes past your face and sticks in the sandy earth.

“What are you doing?” you yell. “It’s me.”

With a look of hatred in his eyes, he pulls his axe from the ground and runs at you, swinging it back and forth with furious strokes.

You raise your sword, blocking his attack and knocking him to the ground. “Zack,” you scream. “Stop it!”

He stands and prepares to swing again, looking much more like a zombie than the friend you have grown up with.

You dodge out of the way of the heavy blade. His axe hits rock, sending up sparks. Drool spills from his open mouth in between short, gurgled breaths. His eyes have a crazed look, and from this short distance you can see that black lines are branching across his face like veins. They continue down to his neck and arms. It must be the poison from the pod.

He swings again, but you block with your sword and knock the axe from his hands. You grab him by the chest plate and shake him, hoping to snap him out of whatever this is.

His eyes remain crazed. His hands snake around your neck, choking you.

Your lungs are screaming for air. If you don't act soon, he will kill you. Swiftly, you bring the hilt of your sword down against his skull. His hands release their hold, and he falls to his knees. You step back, gasping to fill your lungs.

Zack's head is bleeding. He looks up. This time, he seems to recognize you, but he isn't moving. His face is strained like he's struggling to speak.

“What is it?” you ask.

“Run,” he says in a hoarse whisper. Then he moans and curls into a ball. When he lifts his head for the second time the Zack you know is gone again. The veins are concentrated across his face now, and his eyes are completely black. Whatever poisoned him is in control. He grunts and struggles to his feet, stumbling toward his axe.

You know you have to go. You can’t help him, and he *will* kill you. “I’m sorry Zack,” you say. “I’m so sorry.” Without looking back, you run into the trees.

WITHOUT ZACK YOU’RE GOING TO NEED SOME EXTRA HELP. ROLL THE DICE. IF YOU ROLL 2, 5, or 6, YOU GET A HEALING POTION THAT GIVES YOU 10 EXTRA LIFE POINTS.

CHAPTER 16

The battle with Zack has left you weak and shaken. You stumble through the mist-drenched forest for what feels like hours. The fog continues to thicken. You're lost, cold, and horribly alone. This forest was a nightmare before, but without Zack it's even worse.

It will be dark in a few hours. The cave is your only hope, but you have no idea where it is. A quick look at your valor stone tells you there isn't enough energy to call the wolf. You're worried that if you have to spend the night in these woods, it won't be long before you join Zack in the game. What you've fought in the daytime has been bad enough. You're not interested in what comes out at night.

A voice in the distance pulls you from your thoughts. It sounds like a child. You strain to hear it again.

"Please. Someone help me."

It sounds like Ashley. She must have gotten away. You head off through the trees on a run. A low branch catches you across the forehead, but you hardly notice the sting. You have to get to her.

Another voice joins in, begging for help through the dense fog. A flicker of hope swells in your chest. It's Zack. "I'm coming," you yell, but the voices seem to be switching directions.

Just when you think you know which way to go, they shift. The dense fog forms a misty cocoon around you and drapes across the ground like a wet towel. It's impossible to see more than a few feet in front of you.

Kayla's voice stops you. "Don't move." She steps out of the trees right next to you.

You wave her off. "Get away from me. I have to find Ashley and Zack."

The cries for help continue, joined now by a man's voice you don't recognize.

"Don't listen to those voices," she says. "It's a trick."

You start to walk away. "I don't trust any of you anymore!"

Kayla whistles, and Ismael flies at you from the trees. You duck, and he skims the top of your head. The little bird circles around. You prepare for another dive, but this time, he stops short. He hovers in front of you a few feet above the ground and flaps his wings. His strange movements create a gust of air much stronger than it should for such a small bird. The mist around you is temporarily displaced.

Without the fog, you can see you're standing near the edge of a tall cliff. A few more steps, and you would have fallen to your death. Your legs give out, and you sink to the ground. Kayla rushes over as the fog seeps back around you. She helps you scoot away from the cliff's edge.

A series of voices echo through the fog, first Ashley's, then Zack's, then the man's.

Kayla crouches next to you, touching your arm softly. "This place is called the Whispering Woods. The wind is enchanted to make you think you hear the people you love and lure you toward danger."

You look up at her. "And that other voice?"

"It's my dad," she says. Her eyes travel to the ground.

Moments of silence filled with the occasional call for help tick by before she continues. "Where's Zack?"

Her question refuels your anger. "Thanks to your friend, he's been turned into some kind of monster."

Kayla shakes her head. "I didn't know John was going to send you down the wrong path."

"Where is that transparent pile of garbage?"

She hesitates, her eyes filling with tears. "He. . . he faded out. He's gone. . . for good this time."

You aren't sure what to say. You're still angry, but you can tell she's hurting.

"Don't you see?" she says. "That's why he lied to you. He knew I'd be left here alone. I know it's terrible, but he was trying to protect me." Her face crumbles, and droplets start to flow down her cheeks.

Your anger melts. You hate John for what he did to Zack, but you don't want Kayla to be alone, either.

Swallowing around the tightness in your throat, you ask, "So will I be able to see him at least? Now that he's part of the game?"

Her eyes narrow. "Zack?"

"Yeah, does it take a while for him to appear, or will I be able to talk to him today?"

She looks confused. "Zack isn't part of the game."

"I saw him, and believe me, he's gone. A plant blew poison on him, and now he's a zombie or something."

"If he were part of the game, I would know," she says. "I can feel when a new person is absorbed." She looks at you, her face full of hope. "Did this plant have big purple pods and lots of thick vines?"

You nod.

She clasps her hands together "I know the plant you're talking about. It's called black soul. It poisons your mind, but it doesn't kill you. Well, not for a while." She grabs your shoulders and shakes you. "Zack's still alive! If you can beat the game before the poison reaches his heart, you can save him."

You climb to your feet with renewed purpose. "Then I have to make it." You reach for her hand and help her to her feet. "Can you guide me get to the next cave before sundown?"

She nods and blushes a little. "Zack's the sweetest boy I've ever met. I'll do anything I can to help him."

You grin. "Poor Zack. He might never forgive you for saving him."

CHAPTER 17

"It's not much farther," Kayla says.

With her help, you've retraced your steps to where John led you astray. This time, you take the right road to get to the next cave. Ismael circles above you. He scouts the path nearby for danger, then wings his way to Kayla's shoulder.

KAYLA KNOWS WHERE A FLOWER GROWS IN THE FOREST WITH HEALING ABILITIES. IT'S ON THE WAY TO THE CAVE, AND IT MIGHT BE IN BLOOM. ROLL THE DICE. IF YOU ROLL 1 OR 6, YOU FIND THE FLOWER AND GET 5 EXTRA LIFE POINTS.

The landscape has slowly transitioned from thick forest to more of a sandy marsh. The patches of sand shift under your weight, slowing your progress and making it difficult to walk.

She points to a spot on the ground ahead of you. "You're gonna have to watch out for quicksand. If the ground looks wet at all, don't go near it."

"Great," you say. "At this point, the only thing safe is the air."

Kayla makes a face. "Well. . . if you notice a green mist floating around, try not to inhale."

"You're kidding!"

She takes Ismael gently from her shoulder and urges him into the sky. "I wish I were."

You walk along in silence for a few minutes, watching the small hawk ride the air currents. She could use the bird's vision, but then she would fade.

"How long have you been here?" you ask.

She shrugs. "I've lost track, but I think it's been over ten years."

"And no one new has come in?"

"Not 'til you and Zack. I was beginning to wonder if the game was broken, but now I know it's my Dad being amazing."

"Yeah, I guess he kind of is. He's got the whole area fenced off. Zack, Ashley, and I got in by a fluke."

"Ashley? Is that your girlfriend?"

You blush. "No. She's my little sister. The Gamekeeper took her."

Kayla touches your arm. "I had no idea. I'm so sorry."

You take a deep breath, pushing down the

memory of Ashley's frightened face. "I should never have brought her here. She's only five. If I'd listened to her, we'd all be home right now, eating pizza or something."

"You'll save her," Kayla says. "I know you will."

You try to look confident, but deep down, there's a geyser of doubt waiting to erupt. "What about you?" you ask. "Do you have any brothers or sisters?"

"Nope, my mom passed away when I was four. It was just the two of us after that." Her face falls. "My dad's probably so lonely back there without me. You have to get through and let him know I'm okay. Tell him I think he's doing a great job keeping other people out."

It's hard to believe she can be this selfless. "You really don't want other people to be here? Even if it means you'll be all alone?"

"Would you want anyone else trapped in this nightmare?" She adjusts her face into a smile, but you can tell it's difficult. "Besides, I still have Finn. He'll come around."

You stop to rest on a mound of sand. "That reminds me, Finn mentioned something about getting stuck in this world because of a kid. What did he mean by that?"

"Finn wasn't alone in the game," she says. "His younger brother, Jeremy, wandered in, and Finn followed. Finn was a great fighter right from the start. I don't know the whole story, but he got his brother out. He misses the little guy, though, a lot. I think that's the reason he spends so much time alone."

Ismael lets out a warning cry, and the wolf pendant pulses against your chest.

A withered hand rises from under the sand. Gnarled fingers close around your ankle, yanking your leg backward.

You claw at the shifting ground, trying to get away.

Kayla grabs your arm and pulls you to safety.

A hideous creature bursts from the ground with a shriek. It resembles an old woman but with long pointed features and fanged teeth.

"It's a sand hag!" Kayla yells.

The little hawk circles low as you reach for your sword. The hag's tattered robes billow around her as she swipes at you. Kayla launches an arrow, but at the last minute the crone vanishes into a swirl of sand only to materialize to your left. Her dusty cackle rings through the air.

Ismael flies low to strike, but the hag swirls away from him as well.

Kayla is beginning to fade. "Get to the cave," she says as she nocks another arrow. "From there, The Gamekeeper's lair isn't far. I'll find you when I can." She shoots again, this time changing direction at the last moment. Her anticipation of the sand hag's new location is correct. The arrow pierces the creature's arm as she reappears."

Her gravelly scream splits the air, and she charges. Kayla fades before the withered creature can reach her target. With Kayla gone she turns her vengeance on you.

TIME TO BATTLE. ROLL THE DIE.

JUST LIKE BEFORE, MATCH THE NUMBER ON THE DIE TO THE CHART. IF YOU HAVE THE TIME SWORD, A ROLL OF 3 OR HIGHER WILL GIVE YOU ONLY HALF DAMAGE.

IF YOU HAVE THE FIRE SWORD, IT MELTS THE SAND, MAKING IT IMPOSSIBLE FOR HER TO DISAPPEAR. SHE TAKES DOUBLE WOUNDS ON EACH TURN.

IF YOU HAVE THE FROST SWORD, THE HAG RECIEVES ONE EXTRA WOUND ON EACH ROLL.

Roll	1	2	3	4	5	6
Sand Hag Wounds	2	2	3	5	6	6
Your Wounds	4	4	3	2	1	1

THE SAND HAG STARTS WITH FIFTEEN LIFE POINTS. SUBTRACT THE NUMBER OF WOUNDS ACCORDING TO THE CHART AND WRITE IT HERE.

15 - ____=_______.

TRANSFER YOUR LIFE POINTS FROM THE LAST BATTLE PAGE. DON'T FORGET ANY EXTRA LIFE POINTS YOU EARNED. SUBTRACT YOUR WOUNDS AND WRITE IT HERE.(TRANSFERRED POINTS + ANY EXTRA LIFE POINTS- WOUNDS= NEW LIFE POINTS)

________ -_____= ______.

WHEN THE HAG'S POINTS REACH 0, YOU HAVE WON THIS BATTLE. KEEP ROLLING AND SUBTRACTING UNTIL SHE'S DEFEATED. DON'T FORGET TO SUBTRACT YOUR OWN WOUND POINTS FOR EACH ROLL.

GO TO THE LAST PAGE IF YOU RUN OUT OF POINTS. WHEN YOU DEFEAT HER, WRITE THE NUMBER OF POINTS YOU HAVE LEFT HERE ______.

You stagger across the sand. Finally, your legs give out, and you slump to the ground. Kayla said the cave wasn't far from here, but without her you're not sure of the direction. The sun is starting to dip behind the horizon.

You look down at the handle of your sword. The valor stone is full from your battle with the sand hag. The wolf's name forms in your mind. *Gunnolf.* Within minutes you feel his muzzle against your face. "Hey, boy." Relief floods through you at the sight of him. You rub a hand against his chest. "I could use a little help."

The wolf lowers his head and crouches low. He whimpers until you climb onto his back. It surprises you how natural it feels to be there. He rises, and you grab the soft fur around the nape of his neck as he begins to run.

The sun finishes its descent, and an eerie twilight falls upon The Gamekeeper's world.

Gunnolf leaves the sand and returns to the forested path. The sky becomes inky. Snarls, hisses, and moans echo through the trees. There's also a scraping sound you can't place. You remember what

Kayla said about the really bad stuff coming out at night and the horrible visions The Gamekeeper showed you.

Through the darkness, you hear something massive hulking toward you. The wolf gives a low growl. A sliver of moonlight casts a dim glow on a cluster of tall, twisted trees that seem to be moving.

Not swaying-in-the-breeze-moving but walking-toward-you-trying-to-kill-you-moving. A large, wooden fist pummels the ground next to you, spraying wood and dirt everywhere.

The wolf dodges the strike.

You cling tighter to his body.

Beyond the trees, the dim yellow glow of the cave rises out of the darkness. The wolf weaves through the wooden beasts, ducking and dodging the spiked branches and smashing blows.

Your only hope is to get to the cave. The glow from the stone in the cave shines through the darkness. Thirty more feet and you're there. The wolf skillfully maneuvers through the splintering fists and dark creatures until he finally leaps through the entrance of the cave.

A series of bangs, scratches, howls, and roars create a symphony of terror outside the cave. The runes glow around the doorway. They promise safety, at least for the moment.

You slide from the wolf's back. Your muscles feel like cooked spaghetti. You stumble toward the back of the cave to put as much distance as possible between you and the night creatures. Still in your armor, you collapse near the deepest cave wall.

The wolf worries over you, nudging you with his nose. "I'm all right, boy," you say. "Just really tired." You pat his muzzle. "Thanks for coming. You saved me again." Logic tells you to send him away and keep your valor points for another battle. It should be an easy decision, but Zack's absence seems to haunt the cave. You touch the soft fur of his leg. "I know we're safe, but can you stay?"

The wolf circles you twice before he curls up next to you, resting his huge head on his paws. He nudges you again and licks your face. The safety of his massive, furry body next to you relaxes you into a deep sleep.

CHAPTER 18

"Wake up, sleepyhead." A feminine voice pulls you from sleep. As you pry your eyes open, Kayla's freckled nose comes into focus.

Another voice sounds from across the cave. "I still think we should have thrown a bucket of water on him."

"Finn, that's enough," Kayla scolds.

You struggle to your feet, pain flaring in your overused muscles. You look around for the wolf, but he's gone.

Finn sulks against a cave wall not far away.

"Guess I missed a rowdy party last night," Kayla teases, taking in your bloody armor and ripped clothes.

Your lips twist into a rueful grin. "Yeah, it was a real riot."

She points toward the side of the cave. "There's a river over there where you can clean up. Have you looked at the cache yet?"

You shake your head, and new pains jolt through your neck and shoulders.

"He's been too busy cuddled up with his blanky, counting sheep," Finn says. His face is cold and angry.

Kayla puts her hands on her hips. "I told you to be nice—"

"No," you interrupt. "Finn has every right to be mad at me." You turn to him. "I acted like a jerk. You tried to help me, and I wouldn't listen."

"You called me a liar," he says, anger pulsing through each syllable.

You stare at your shoes. "I know. The Gamekeeper messed with my head, and I figured. . ."

"You figured that because I'd rather not join the walking dead pep club," he says, gesturing to Kayla, "that I'd be the one to lead you into a trap."

Your shoulders lift slightly. "Well, yeah."

"The Gamekeeper did come to me," he says, pushing off the wall and stalking toward you. "He tried to get me to lead you into trouble. He offered me a lot of things, but I wouldn't do it."

Having to admit this is your fault feels like a punch to the gut. "I made a bad call. Trust me, I'm paying for it. I chose to listen to John, and now Zack is . . . well I'm not even really sure what he is."

The mention of Zack's condition seems to settle Finn's temper. His demeanor softens. "Don't you realize if you morons die in this place, I'm stuck with you for like the next fifty years?" He nods toward Kayla. "This one's enough of a pain."

"Finn wasn't keen on helping," she explains. "I hung around all night, talking as much as I could, until he finally agreed to come here and talk to you."

Finn watches as you try to scrub the grime from your hands and face in the river. He looks at his feet. "I'm sorry about what happened to your friend. It looks like you've more than suffered for doubting me."

You use the edge of your shirt to dry your face as you stand. "Is that enough to get you to help?"

Finn winks. "It's a start."

Kayla pushes between you, waving a hand as if to clear the air. "Okay, now that we have all the male bonding out of the way, let's get down to business. I have a plan that can get both you and Zack home before dinner."

Your head snaps in her direction. "Did you find

Zack? Where is he?"

Kayla nods. "I've been following him through the forest. The creatures seem to leave him alone. I guess because of the poison. It's strange, but it seems like he recognizes me sometimes."

This comment makes you smile. It's just like Zack to have his hormones course stronger through his brain than a soul-sucking poison.

"So, what's this plan of yours?" Finn asks.

She tilts her head toward him. "You're going to help?"

He nods. "If that's what it takes to get rid of them, I'm in. Besides, I'd love to see the look on The Gamekeeper's face when someone gets the better of him."

Kayla throws her arms around Finn and jumps up and down. He pretends to be disgusted, but the corners of his mouth split into a brief smile.

She steps back and composes herself. Picking up a stick, she draws a crude map in the dirt of the cave floor. "So, we're super close to The Gamekeeper's castle. You'll get there by this afternoon if you stay on the path. It's not going to be easy. He's going to send everything he has at you. I've seen him with your sister, and he really seems to like her."

"You've seen Ashley, too?" you blurt out.

Crimson creeps into her cheeks. "I'm pretty determined once I set my mind to something."

"That's the understatement of the year," Finn says. "She talked non-stop for two hours to get me to come here. She even sang show tunes." His face contorts with disgust. "It was horrible."

"Anyway," Kayla cuts in. "Ashley's fine. I couldn't get too close, but The Gamekeeper's treating her well. The harder she fights him, the more delighted he seems with her."

"Do you think we can get her out?" you ask.

Her eyes light up. "That's the best part. He's holding her in a room at the back of his castle. The portal to send you home is in that same room. If you can get to her, and get through, you win the game and can go home."

"They're in the same room? It seems too easy," you say.

Finn speaks up. "The Gamekeeper probably doesn't believe you'll ever make it that far. His biggest weakness is his overconfidence."

"What about Zack?" you ask.

"I'll bring him to the castle," Kayla says. She looks at the floor and tries to hide a shy smile. "I know he'll follow me."

Finn steps forward. "Where do I come in?"

"You help in the battle as long as possible," she says. "Between the two of you . . ." She glances at your valor stone. ". . . and the wolf, you should be able to fight your way to the castle."

You wonder if she knows you used up your valor tokens keeping the wolf with you last night.

"Now," she continues, "let's go look at that cache."

You walk toward the glowing jewel protruding from the back wall of the cave. In the recess below it, there's another sack of the crackers and a pouch with some bright red berries.

ROLL THE DICE. IF YOU GET EITHER 3 OR 5, THESE BERRIES WILL GIVE YOU 5 EXTRA LIFE POINTS.

Along with the food in the cache, there is a collection of helmets. Your fingers tingle as you get close to one made of silver with an image of a wolf howling. Picking it up, you notice that there is a small indentation in the front.

"That's strange," Kayla says, rubbing a finger over the small space. "It's like a jewel or something fell out."

The pendant pulses at your chest, and you pull it from your neck. You hold the brass wolf's eye up to the helmet. It's a perfect fit. Through the eye, you can see that the indent seems to glow with the same blue light at your valor stone. You slide the pendant from the chain and place it in the indent.

"You've had that the whole time?" Finn asks.

"Almost," you say. "We found it in the second cache." You don the helmet. "Whoa." You look around the cave, seeing its true nature for the first time. "There are words scrawled everywhere in blue light across the cave walls. It looks like the light from my valor stone. I've never seen this language before."

"They must be protective spells," Kayla says. "Somehow, between the helmet and stone, you can see the magic that's been cast for protection here."

You continue to scan the cave. Kayla and Finn

are both bathed in the same blue light as the walls, and it radiates from your armor.

"This is amazing," you tell them. "The Gamekeeper makes it seem like this is his world, but there's lots of other magic here too." You take the helmet off, and the cave returns to normal. "Let's hope it's enough."

Chapter 19

After recuperating in the cave until sunrise, you pack up your supplies and gather your armor. Your muscles don't hurt anymore, and the fatigue that plagued you last night seems to have evaporated.

Maybe it's the power of the cave or the unusual crackers from the cache, but you feel ready to take on the next challenge. Well, as ready as you can be to take on a psychotic bad-guy who controls all the evil in the world you're trapped in.

Kayla heads out to find Zack while you and Finn start your journey toward The Gamekeeper's castle. Bits of splintered wood— mementos of your battle with the tree creatures—litter the ground outside the cave entrance.

Several sets of tracks mar the muddy ground beyond the barrier of the rune stones. Some appear to be from large hooves. Some tracks ooze with slime, and others you can't even identify. The one that makes your skin crawl the most is the unmistakable twisting imprint of a large snake.

"Geez," Finn says, looking around. "Was there

anything that didn't come after you last night? This looks like a line for an all-that-could-eat-you-buffet."

You examine another set of tracks that look like they belong to some species of large cat. Kayla shudders, and you remember how she got stuck in the game.

Glancing around, you realize just how many creatures were out to get you. "I thought fighting blind last night was horrible, but now I'm grateful for the dark." You scan the trees cautiously, but there doesn't seem to be any immediate threat.

Following Finn's lead, you start down the winding path that leads away from the cave. Other than a few small lizards that shoot barbs from their tongues and some bushes that burst into flames if you touch them, the forest is relatively quiet for miles.

The lizards are easily spooked and run away without much resistance. The bushes are another story. Finn demonstrates how to recognize the unique, diamond shape of their leaves, so you can avoid them and save your eyebrows.

You stop to catch your breath. "It seems too easy. Why haven't we had to fight anything big here?"

"It's too close to The Gamekeeper's castle," Finn says. He gestures for you to follow him to the top of a small hill. From the higher ground, you can see the cold, black stone of the fortress shadowed against the distant horizon.

Everything about this new place seems to be poisoned by The Gamekeeper's evil. For miles, the vines and trees surrounding his home are withered and dark. The land looks dead. Cursed. Your stomach twists, but Ashley is there, and Zack doesn't have much time left. A mental image of him with those black veins running across his face is enough to push you forward with greater determination.

Throughout this part of the terrain, there is a new kind of insect. Finn calls them jewel crickets. When spooked, they fly into the air, spinning like a top and emitting a high-pitched whistle.

They produce a colorful shower of sparks that change colors as they spin. No two seem to spark the same colors. Some start out green and spin to blue and then red. Some are purple first before switching to gold and then orange. You might think they were beautiful if they weren't so annoying.

Throughout the day, these pesky insects have spooked you several times. Even though you know they are harmless, it still makes you jump, and their whistle hurts your ears. You have grown to dislike them immensely.

At the top of the hill, you put on the helmet. It shows you where there are concentrations of dark magic, and you're able to avoid The Gamekeeper's traps. As you climb through the dark landscape, weaving in and out of spiked plants and lava pits, you wonder about the last time Finn was here. "Was it this hard when you got near The Gamekeeper?"

His jaw tightens. "Everything was harder because I had Jeremy with me."

"Jeremy? Your brother?"

Finn nods. Deep sadness etches his face, and you're about to change the subject when he answers. "He was only eight, but he was a tough kid." A memory seems to come to mind, and he smiles wistfully. "He was barely as big as his axe, but he fought right beside Sampson and me through the whole thing." He pauses and then says abruptly. "We should hurry. Watch where you put your feet."

You climb over a withered tree and follow a makeshift path as it winds through a field of large toadstools.

"Don't let them touch your skin," Finn says. Your flesh will rot away wherever they touch you."

Though they look normal to your naked eye, the helmet's power reveals the toadstools are dripping a vile black liquid, and a dark vapor rises from them. You direct Finn to cover his nose and mouth with his shirt, and you do the same to avoid breathing in the questionable fumes.

After carefully navigating through the toadstools, you steer Finn around an area that appears as a strange, hazy shadow through the helmet. When you throw a rock at the area, the ground falls away to expose a giant sink hole with jagged rocks at the bottom.

You stop to rest. The jewel crickets buzz around you, spinning and buzzing like an electric flower garden. They're actually quite pretty when they're not jumping out of a bush and scaring you to death with their high-pitched whir. You take a drink from your canteen, and then offer it to Finn.

He waves it off. "I don't really need the water. You should save it."

You insist. The look on his face as you offer it again tells you it's about more than the water.

"Thanks," he says, taking a small swig. "I won't die without it, but it does feel good to have a drink, like I'm almost human again."

"How did it happen?" The words fly out of your mouth, and you're unsure how to take it back, so you keep going. "When you became part of the game, I mean. Was it The Gamekeeper?"

He takes a drink from the canteen before answering. "Jeremy and I made it all the way to the end. There was this giant bull creature I thought for sure was going to pulverize us, but we made it. Sampson helped a lot. Jeremy thought a huge ram was the greatest pet ever. He practically worshipped him."

Frustration creeps into his expression. "I'm still not sure what happened. At the back of the castle, in the throne room, we could see the portal. Just as Jeremy started to walk through, I felt something drop down on us. I blocked him with my body, and then I felt a stinging pain in my neck." He passes the canteen back to you and resumes walking, so you follow.

"The next thing I knew, I was back in the middle of the forest with Sampson. I looked for Jeremy for days. It wasn't until I faded out for the first time that I had to face facts. Jeremy was gone."

"At least you know he's safe."

Finn nodded. "Yeah, and I'm grateful, but everything here reminds me of him. We should never have been here. Jeremy and I should have grown up together. Instead, because of The Gamekeeper's tricks, we're both alone."

As you come to a clearing, Finn pulls you behind a group of large boulders. The Gamekeeper's castle is only about a hundred yards away. Finn points toward the main gate, and, following his gesture, you see a small army of flying bat-like creatures circling above the entrance.

You sink further behind the rock. "I think that's what took Ashley."

Finn nods. "That's the Vargull. They're another of The Gamekeeper's personal protection."

"At least they're not flesh hounds."

Finn lowers his voice. "No, they're worse."

"How?" you ask. "They just look like big bats"

"More like enormous bats with razor sharp teeth, huge hooked claws, and nasty attitudes. Oh, and I forgot to mention their diet."

You swallow, trying to control the bile that builds in your throat. "You're going to tell me they drink blood, aren't you?"

Finn smiles. "Yep."

"So, to save Ashley and Zack and get back home, all I have to do is beat an army of blood-sucking bats the size of ice cream trucks?"

"That and whatever else The Gamekeeper's got up his sleeve. Remember I never saw the creature that took me out."

You process what Finn is telling you. "How did you get past these things with Jeremy?"

"I didn't have to. This is all for you." Finn gives a little chuckle. "These guys hardly ever leave the castle. You must have really made The Gamekeeper mad ."

You squint toward the entrance. "If I'm going to donate blood, I think I'd rather contact the Red Cross. Do you think we could sneak in?"

"We can try. It's a pretty slim chance they won't see us, though. Plus, I think they kind of sense you, you know? After I lost the game, the creatures didn't seem so set on killing me. Oh, they'd come at me if I provoked them, but they didn't hunt me anymore like they did when I was human."

You look up again at the many Vargull circling the castle, silhouetted against the setting sun. "I thought bats didn't like the light."

"They don't, but it seems they made an exception for you. I doubt it put them in a better mood."

"Why haven't they attacked yet?"

"Not sure, but I have a theory. You know the saying blind as a bat? Well, it fits here. They really are almost completely blind."

An idea comes to mind, and you're thankful that you paid attention in science class. "Do they use sonar to find their prey like regular bats?"

"I think so."

Despite the dismal surroundings and huge flying death machines, you smile. "We may have a better chance of sneaking into that castle than I thought."

CHAPTER 20

The area below the castle, where you and Finn are hidden, is covered with short, leafy bushes. From here, you can see the castle doors as well as the Vargull circling high above.

Finn looks down at himself with disgust. "This is gross."

You've both covered yourselves in mud. Pieces of decomposing leaves and bark scratch against your skin through the cold, slimy goop. The swampy, sulfur-tinged aroma makes you gag, but you hope the mud will act as camouflage. A shrill, almost deafening whirr comes from inside your backpack.

"Aaagh." Finn puts a muddy hand over the ear closest to you. "Those things are killing me."

You can barely hear him over the sound of the twenty-five or so jewel crickets currently residing in your backpack. You had to backtrack to catch them, but it was worth the lost time. "I know. They're terrible, but look." You point to the Vargull that are now flapping around wildly.

"They don't look happy," Finn says.

"No, they don't. The crickets seem to be agitating them. If I'm right, they should completely throw off the Vargulls' sonar. We'll be invisible."

Finn flips a piece of dripping mud from his fingertips. "If we're blocking their sonar, why do we need to be covered in mud?"

"To block what they see with their regular vision."

"We don't even know if they have regular vision."

You narrow your eyes. "They want to use me as a human juice box, so I'm not taking any chances." You dart from bush to bush, closing in on the castle's front doors. The crickets are quiet now, but the Vargull become restless as you approach.

"They must sense you're close," Finn says.

You slip off your backpack. "Time to deploy the secret weapon." Carefully, you unzip the pack, doing your best not to set the crickets off. "Call Sampson," you say.

The ram appears. Hopefully, your plan will take effect before they see him. You hook your open pack around one of his horns and point toward the castle door. "Go for it, Sampson. Get to the doors."

He runs toward the protected entryway, scattering crickets in his wake. The jewel crickets click and spin in a flurry of bright colors and noise.

"Look!" Finn points to the sky. "It's working."

The Vargulls' uniform circle has turned into a scattered panic. One bat even hits a tree, tangling himself among the branches. The large beast cries out in distress, adding to the noise and confusion. The chaos seems to spur more colorful flights from the crickets.

You and Finn rush toward the castle. Sampson is battering the door over and over. His persistence pays off. It bends and then splinters. He pushes himself into the tiled foyer. Light spills across the darkened courtyard.

"Don't know why they're so upset. Sampson totally knocked first," Finn says with a wink.

A rush of air beats behind you. Finn pulls you to the ground as a clawed wing slices through the air where your head used to be.

Three Vargull land in front of the breached doorway. They screech and pace back and forth, serving as giant guard dogs. Their milky eyes search for you. Their fangs drip saliva.

Finn doesn't grab his daggers this time. Instead, he pulls out a slingshot and some round papery balls, each the size of a small orange.

The bat-creatures are disoriented, but they snap and claw viciously at the air in front of them. Though they can't see you, they seem to know you're here. More have landed behind you. You're surrounded.

Slowly you draw your sword. You rush forward, swinging your blade, and slash a deep gouge across the nearest beast. It screeches and flails before finally slumping to the ground.

Finn begins to sling the little balls, which turn out to be exploding rounds. A well-timed shot sends two of the bats to the ground.

You look at the hilt of your sword. "My valor stone isn't too far from full. The wolf will be here soon."

Sampson reappears from the castle and uses his horns to knock two Vargull to the ground. One of Finn's rounds finishes them off.

"Atta boy, Sampson," Finn yells.

One of the large bats soars by you.

Reaching up, you slice its wing with your sword. The creature rolls through the air and smacks into the building. It pulls itself up and starts to claw its way toward you. Another Vargull knocks you to the ground from behind. The crawling beast is right on top of you.

A flash of blue light from Sampson's supercharged horns throws the Vargull against the wall. A second blast leaves the creature sizzling and dead.

A glance toward Finn tells you he's starting to fade.

"Thank you, Finn," you yell. "I'll find a way to get you out of here. I promise."

Finn nods. "I'll hold you to that." He sends another three successful rounds at the enemy before he and Sampson fade completely.

A raptor-like claw slashes your arm and knocks your sword to the ground. You scramble over to grab it. Searing pain rips through your leg as another claw slices across it.

You lunge for the sword. With your hand around

the hilt, you roll onto your back and hack at anything that comes near you. The smell of your blood seems to have drawn the colony. They have you pinned down.

You feel a pulse from the pendant stone now residing in your helmet. A trumpeting howl echoes through the night air. The Vargull scatter back to the sky.

Gunnolf stands over your body, snapping at the bats as they dive. He snatches one from the air by a leg and gives it several bone-crushing shakes before tossing its lifeless body to the side.

You roll to your feet next to the wolf and face the circling enemy. Through the trees, you catch a glimpse of Kayla and Zack in the forest below the castle. She kept her promise and brought him to the castle. They can make it inside if clear the path for them.

You give Gunnolf a quick pat. "We can do this!" You glance at Zack stumbling through the brush and softly add, "We have to."

The Vargull swarm above you, ready to attack.

THE STAKES ARE HIGH.

IT'S TIME TO ROLL THE DIE. REMEMBER, YOU NEED TO MATCH THE NUMBER ON THE DIE TO THE CHART. IF YOU HAVE THE FROST SWORD OR THE ELEMENTAL BLADE, DOUBLE THE WOUNDS TO THE VARGULL ON A 3 OR 5.

IF YOU HAVE THE SHADOW SWORD, IT HELPS CLOAK YOU FROM THE VARGULL. SUBTRACT ONLY HALF POINTS ON A ROLL OF 1 OR 2.

Roll	1	2	3	4	5	6
Vargull Wounds	1	2	3	4	5	6
Your Wounds	6	6	4	3	1	1

THE VARGULL START WITH 20 LIFE POINTS. SUBTRACT THE WOUNDS THEY

GET ACCORDING TO THE CHART AND WRITE IT HERE

20 - ____=_______.

TRANSFER YOUR LIFE POINTS FROM THE BOTTOM OF THE LAST BATTLE PAGE AND WRITE IT HERE ____.

SUBTRACT THE NUMBER OF WOUNDS YOU TOOK ACCORDING TO THE ROLL. (TRANSFERRED POINTS+ EXTRA LIFE POINTS - WOUNDS= NEW LIFE POINTS)

_______ -_____= ______.

IF THE VARGULLS' POINTS REACH 0, YOU HAVE WON THIS BATTLE. IF THEY STILL HAVE POINTS LEFT, KEEP ROLLING AND SUBTRACTING UNTIL THEY ARE DEFEATED.

IF YOU RUN OUT OF POINTS GO TO THE LAST PAGE.

WHEN YOU DEFEAT THEM, WRITE THE NUMBER OF POINTS YOU HAVE LEFT HERE ________ TO USE FOR FUTURE BATTLES.

CHAPTER 21

You sit in front of the splintered door and wait for Zack and Kayla. The Vargull you didn't kill have flown off. You can make out the shape of their large wings against the horizon. The castle sits silently, but you're sure The Gamekeeper knows you're here. The wolf paces back and forth. He gives a low growl, and you immediately pull out your sword and grab your helmet.

Kayla appears from behind the bushes, leading Zack. He's bound around his chest with a thick rope that pins his arms against his sides.

Gunnolf growls again.

"It's okay, boy," she says to the wolf. "It's just us."

In a trance-like state, Zack follows behind Kayla. The black veins are bigger now, branching wildly across his neck and face. His eyes are vacant and bulging. His mouth hangs open.

As soon as he sees you, he growls and rushes toward you. Kayla restrains him with the long rope in her hands. "He's pretty weak from the poison, but he'll still come after you if you give him the chance.."

Zack thrashes against the rope and snaps at you with his teeth.

"Did he give you much trouble?" you ask.

Kayla turns Zack away from you, so he'll calm down. "No. He follows me wherever I go if I walk slow enough. I don't understand why he doesn't try to attack me, but I'm thankful for it." She takes a bandana out of her pocket and carefully puts it across Zack's mouth, so he can't hurt you. He stares at her face and makes a soft grunting sound.

"I think I know why," you say under your breath.

Kayla quickly changes the subject. "I've never been to the castle before."

"Not even when you were a player in the game?"

She laughs. "I didn't really make it that far. Before I got stuck here, I wasn't exactly the warrior type."

But you're amazing with that bow and arrow."

She blows out a puff of air. "Yeah, *now* I am. There's not a lot of things to do around here. What I wouldn't give for a movie theater." Her eyes light up at the thought. "And a cheeseburger. I miss that the most. Well, that and my Dad." Her face grows serious. "You won't forget to talk to him? He needs to know that I'm okay."

You draw an X across your chest with your finger. "I promise. I would never have made it through this place without you, Ismael, and Finn."

"John, too?" Kayla asks timidly.

You think for a moment and then shrug. "John, too. I suppose I can forgive him. He didn't want you to be alone. I get it. Plus, he came with an enormous bear. That had to help a little."

The wolf paces back and forth. His ears stand high, and he's panting. He gives a small whine whenever he walks near the castle doors.

You look around for any signs of danger but see nothing. "I wonder what's wrong with him."

Kayla looks at the ground. "We can't go in. I can feel some kind of force field the closer we get to the door." She throws her arms around you. "I'm so sorry you're here, but I am glad that you came. It's the first bit of hope I've had in a long time." She hands you the end of Zack's rope. "I guess this is goodbye." She walks over to Zack and kisses him on the cheek.

She squeezes your arm gently, "Take care of him."

You nod.

She walks down the castle steps toward the forest. Turning back, she gives a small wave and then fades away.

The wolf lies down at your feet. You kneel beside him and scratch his silky head. The tightness in your throat makes it hard to talk. "Zack was right about you all along, wasn't he?" The wolf gives a small whimper and licks at the tears that snake down your cheeks.

You lay your head against his. "We did it, boy. Because of you, we made it to the castle. You're the best Guardian in the world." Sniffing, you wipe your nose across your sleeve. "Now I have to finish this on my own." You run your hand across his head one more time and then pat his back.

The wolf seems to understand. He rises, nuzzles his head against your leg, and then, he too fades away.

After a deep breath, you pick up your helmet and pull your friend through the splintered doorway. Without Kayla around, Zack is harder to control.

Several times, he tries to attack you, but he's too weak to do much damage, especially all tied up. Your footsteps echo across the cold obsidian floors of a narrow hallway. Eventually, it opens into an extravagant throne room.

Two large granite thrones sit side by side on a raised platform. The Gamekeeper reclines on one, and Ashley sits curled in a defiant ball in the other.

"Ashley!" You drop Zack's rope and rush toward her.

Her face brightens, and she jumps up to greet you. Just as she leaves the chair, black ropes shoot from the armrests. They wrap tightly around her and pull her back. She starts to scream, and more ropes circle her mouth.

The Gamekeeper smirks. "Aaah, you're just in time for tea." He snaps his fingers, and two stubby goblin-like creatures rush out, snorting and spitting. They carry a heavy tray piled high with cups, teapots, and cakes.

You grip your helmet tightly. "I don't want tea. I want my sister, and I want to go home."

"Are you sure?" He gestures toward Zack, who is

wandering around the back of the room. "Your friend doesn't look so good."

"He's fine. Now get those creepy ropes off my sister, and let us go." You put your helmet on and feel a pulse from the wolf's eye pendant. The scene before you looks very different through the magic of the helmet. The bonds that hold Ashley glow red, which must be The Gamekeeper's magic because he is also surrounded by a red glow.

Behind him is a huge swirling vortex enclosed in a circle of runes. Red and blue light twists and spins around the black hole at the center. It must be the portal home. Remembering Finn's story, you look around for the invisible beast.

The Gamekeeper is going on about hospitality and his "little family." From the corner of your eye, you see a movement near the ceiling, against an upper window. Slowly, a creature starts to unfurl and descend from the ceiling. You try not to let on that you see it.

"We made it through your game," you say, positioning yourself across from Ashley. "Time to keep your end of the bargain."

He waves off your comment. “In due time. . . in due time. Can’t we talk for a bit? Rush, rush, rush.” He shakes his head disapprovingly. “You young people, always in such a hurry. No time for courtesy.” He continues to talk as the creature’s shadowy form comes closer. It drops to the floor behind the throne The Gamekeeper is lounging in.

You fight to keep your face neutral, so The Gamekeeper won’t know you can see it. As the creature slinks around the granite chair, you see that its torso is that of a pale woman dressed in black leather, but the large bulbous body and legs are those of a huge white spider. Her black eyes glisten against her chalky skin. She licks her ruby lips greedily, exposing two horrible fangs.

The Gamekeeper drones on. “Stay,” he says. “Stay here with me. Enjoy my hospitality. Be part of my family. You’ve already won. You can travel home anytime you want. I get lonely here day after day with only goblins for company. Put down your weapons and armor and rest for a while. He gestures around the throne room. “As you can see, it’s perfectly safe.”

The spidery woman continues to creep toward

you, her spindly legs gliding silently across the floor. She's a walking nightmare, and it's taking everything inside you to pretend you don't see her.

She's nearly on top of you when you take your sword from its scabbard, struggling to keep your voice from shaking. "I don't want to fight anymore," you say to The Gamekeeper. You hold your sword in front of you as if you are about to lay it down at his feet. Just as it touches the cold stone of the platform, you swing it up and spin to the left. It slices through the air and severs the spider-lady's head from her body.

The hideous, fanged head rolls to a final resting place near The Gamekeeper's feet. Blood pours from her convulsing body. The invisibility is gone. Ashley's face pales as the huge, headless spider-lady becomes visible. The portal is also now visible as well.

All of the goblins screech and run from the room, leaving a trail of dishes behind them.

The Gamekeeper's eyes narrow and his lips form a thin line.

Your voice echoes through the hall. "NO MORE GAMES!" Sword lifted, you step toward him as an imposing warrior. "You have been beaten. Give me my sister, and let us pass."

The Gamekeeper gives a moody wave of his hand, and Ashley's bindings disappear.

She rushes forward and throws her arms around you. "I knew you would come." She hugs you tightly for a moment. "Uhh, what's wrong with Zack?" she asks as he staggers toward you, apparently drawn by the portal.

He can barely stand. The black veins strain through his pale skin. He doesn't even try to attack you anymore.

You need to get him through the portal soon. You pull his rope and start to lead him and Ashley around the thrones, well away from The Gamekeeper's reach. You keep your sword pointed at the evil man.

"You're right," The Gamekeeper says through clenched teeth. "You have beaten me, and so you are free to go home." He makes a dramatic sweeping gesture toward the portal.

You continue around the throne until you stand directly in front of the swirling portal.

"I just hope they have a cure for the effects of Black Soul in your world. I find it highly unlikely, but at least your friend won't suffer long."

You turn toward him. "What do you mean? You said if I got through your game, we could go home. I've done everything you asked. Zack will be fine when we get through the portal."

"Well, if by fine you mean. . . that." He gestures to Zack. "I suppose you are correct. But if you'd like him healthy and normal again, perhaps we could make a deal for a cure." His eyes light up at the idea.

You shake your head. "Your deals are always bad ones."

The Gamekeeper's lips form into an arrogant grin. He turns his hand over, and a teardrop-shaped bottle full of swirling black liquid appears in his palm. "This is the only known cure for the poison."

"What's the catch?" you say.

"No catch. Just a negotiation, a business deal if you will. I'll give you the potion, and you can have your little friend healthy and whole. In exchange, you promise to come back and play this game again—at a time of *my* choosing."

You swallow hard. The portal is so close. All you need to do is step through, and you're out of this nightmare. Zack falls to his knees. You want to scream—or cry. This is so unfair. You did everything right.

You clench your fists. "I want proof it will work."

The Gamekeeper smiles as if he knows he's got you. "Fine, but if it does, then do we have an agreement?"

You take a deep breath, feeling the crushing weight of your actions. With a heavy heart, you nod.

The Gamekeeper hands the bottle to one of his goblins, and it runs over to you. It squeezes three drops into Zack's gasping mouth and runs away.

Zack continues to moan and pant.

"Nothing's happening."

"Patience, dear boy," The Gamekeeper says, picking at his nails.

A moment passes, and then Zack starts to convulse. You and Ashley drop to your knees next to him. After a moment, he stops moving.

Ashley starts to cry.

You look up at The Gamekeeper in horror. "You killed him!"

The dark man laughs. "Now where's the fun in that?"

Suddenly, Zack gasps. The black veins recede from his face and then disappear. He opens his eyes. "Where am I?" He notices the ropes around his body and turns to you. "I get the feeling I missed something." His voice is scratchy and weak, but he's back to his old self.

"Not much," you answer. "I'll fill you in when we get home." You use your sword to cut through the ropes. You send Zack and then Ashley through the portal.

When they are both safely through, you step forward to take your turn.

"Don't forget," The Gamekeeper calls after you. "I'll be expecting you—very soon."

Once you step through the portal, your world comes into focus. You're back on the path where you first met The Gamekeeper. Your clothes are still ripped and muddy, but you're home, and you're safe. At least for now. The armor you had is gone. You look over and see Zack's is gone as well.

"We made it!" He yells, and he and Ashley throw their arms around you.

"Yeah." You sigh. "We made it." You look over your shoulder and see the last of the vortex close and disappear. It feels so good to be home. You're not even going to think about The Gamekeeper. He could come for you tomorrow or in twenty years. The important thing is you beat him.

A pulse from your chest surprises you, and you look down to see the wolf pendant hanging there. Although you know that you'll have to fight The Gamekeeper again soon, at least you know you won't have to do it alone. *Take care, Gunnolf*, you think. As if in answer, the pendant pulses again.

You, Zack, and Ashley run toward home. At the fork, you high five Zack and tell him you'll see him tomorrow.

"Are you ever going to tell me about the ropes?" he asks.

You laugh. "Maybe someday. You pause, knowing that your next sentence is a loaded one. "I might even tell you about how Kayla kissed you."

He does a double take. "Kayla did what?"

You take Ashley's hand and start down the final stretch home.

Zack calls after you. "Aw, come on, man. You can't throw that out there and not tell me more. What's the matter with you?"

You wave and keep walking.

Ashley pulls at your sleeve.

You look down at her. Her little face seems so serious that you're almost afraid to ask. "What's up, squirt?"

She drags her toe through the dirt. "I know you saved me and all, and I'm super grateful, but. . ." She takes a deep breath. "I'm totally going to tell Mom about this."

You scoop her up in your arms and swing her around. "I wouldn't have it any other way."

LAST PAGE (ONLY IF YOU'VE RUN OUT OF LIFE POINTS.) IF YOU'RE HERE, THEN YOU'VE RUN OUT OF LIFE POINTS, AND YOUR GAME HAS ENDED. I TOLD YOU THIS WASN'T GOING TO BE EASY.

THE GAMEKEEPER NEEDS TO BE BEATEN, SO I'LL MAKE YOU A DEAL. I'LL GIVE YOU A SPECIAL POTION THAT WILL GIVE YOU A SECOND CHANCE TO TAKE HIM OUT. GO BACK TO THE BATTLE WHERE YOU WERE DEFEATED. THIS NEW POTION GIVES YOU TWENTY LIFE POINTS TO START AGAIN.

YOU WILL BECOME PART OF THE GAME IF YOU RUN OUT OF LIFE POINTS A SECOND TIME. DON'T GIVE UP. YOU CAN'T LET THE GAMEKEEPER WIN. YOU CAN ALWAYS START THE BOOK AGAIN. EVERY TIME THROUGH IS A DIFFERENT EXPERIENCE. KEEP FIGHTING AND GOOD LUCK.

ABOUT THE AUTHORS

Ann Acton is the author of the Miracle Maker (Covenant Book, 2016) that was made into a feature length film. (Mainstay Productions, 2015) She has been writing professionally for a number of years and is a member of the Society of Children's Book Writers and Illustrators, as well as two other national writing organizations.

Brenick Acton loves video games, basketball, and hanging out with friends, family, and his dog Ragnar. Although this is his first book, he has been building worlds and telling stories of adventure his whole life.